Praise for th
Kate

"Sitting Marsh and i_____
realistically and humorously depicted."
—*The Mystery Reader*

"Likable characters, period details, and a puzzle that
kept me guessing until the end . . . Very enjoyable."
—*Mystery News*

"Clever and cunning . . . Delightfully unique and enter-
taining. A most delicious tea-time mystery with just the
right atmosphere and a charming cast of characters."
—*The Literary Times*

"Delightful and charming."　　　—*Painted Rock Reviews*

"Well-drawn characters."　　　—*Publishers Weekly*

"Full of humor, suspense, adventure, and touches of
romance . . . delightful."　　　—*Rendezvous*

"A fun-to-read historical mystery." —*Midwest Book Review*

"Trust me, you will not be disappointed . . . Ms. Kingsbury has created a memorable series with delightful
characters that can be enjoyed over and over again."
—*MyShelf.com*

"Sublime . . . Fascinating mid-twentieth-century mystery."
—*BookBrowser*

"[Kingsbury's] characters are strongly drawn, and she
knows the tensions that underlie the calm and soothing
surface of an English village."
—*Salem (OR) Statesman Journal*

Visit Kate Kingsbury's website at
www.doreenrobertshight.com

Manor House Mysteries by Kate Kingsbury

A BICYCLE BUILT FOR MURDER
DEATH IS IN THE AIR
FOR WHOM DEATH TOLLS
DIG DEEP FOR MURDER
PAINT BY MURDER
BERRIED ALIVE
FIRE WHEN READY
WEDDING ROWS
AN UNMENTIONABLE MURDER

Pennyfoot Hotel Mysteries by Kate Kingsbury

ROOM WITH A CLUE
DO NOT DISTURB
SERVICE FOR TWO
EAT, DRINK, AND BE BURIED
CHECK-OUT TIME
GROUNDS FOR MURDER
PAY THE PIPER
CHIVALRY IS DEAD
RING FOR TOMB SERVICE
DEATH WITH RESERVATIONS
DYING ROOM ONLY
MAID TO MURDER
NO CLUE AT THE INN

AN
UNMENTIONABLE
MURDER

KATE KINGSBURY

BERKLEY PRIME CRIME, NEW YORK

THE BERKLEY PUBLISHING GROUP
Published by the Penguin Group
Penguin Group (USA) Inc.
375 Hudson Street, New York, New York 10014, USA

Penguin Group (Canada), 90 Eglinton Avenue East, Suite 700, Toronto, Ontario M4P 2Y3, Canada
(a division of Pearson Penguin Canada Inc.)
Penguin Books Ltd., 80 Strand, London WC2R 0RL, England
Penguin Group Ireland, 25 St. Stephen's Green, Dublin 2, Ireland (a division of Penguin Books Ltd.)
Penguin Group (Australia), 250 Camberwell Road, Camberwell, Victoria 3124, Australia
(a division of Pearson Australia Group Pty. Ltd.)
Penguin Books India Pvt. Ltd., 11 Community Centre, Panchsheel Park, New Delhi—110 017, India
Penguin Group (NZ), Cnr. Airborne and Rosedale Roads, Albany, Auckland 1310, New Zealand
(a division of Pearson New Zealand Ltd.)
Penguin Books (South Africa) (Pty.) Ltd., 24 Sturdee Avenue, Rosebank, Johannesburg 2196,
South Africa

Penguin Books Ltd., Registered Offices: 80 Strand, London WC2R 0RL, England

This is a work of fiction. Names, characters, places, and incidents either are the product of the author's imagination or are used fictitiously, and any resemblance to actual persons, living or dead, business establishments, events, or locales is entirely coincidental. The publisher does not have any control over and does not assume any responsibility for author or third-party websites or their content.

PUBLISHER'S NOTE: The recipes contained in this book are to be followed exactly as written. The publisher is not responsible for your specific health or allergy needs that may require medical supervision. The publisher is not responsible for any adverse reactions to the recipes contained in this book.

AN UNMENTIONABLE MURDER

A Berkley Prime Crime Book / published by arrangement with the author

PRINTING HISTORY
Berkley Prime Crime mass-market edition / August 2006

Copyright © 2006 by Doreen Roberts Hight.
Cover illustration by Dan Craig.
Cover design by Elaine Groh.

ISBN: 0-425-21114-2

BERKLEY® PRIME CRIME
Berkley Prime Crime Books are published by The Berkley Publishing Group,
a division of Penguin Group (USA) Inc.,
375 Hudson Street, New York, New York 10014.
The name BERKLEY PRIME CRIME and the BERKLEY PRIME CRIME design are trademarks belonging to Penguin Group (USA) Inc.

PRINTED IN THE UNITED STATES OF AMERICA

10 9 8 7 6 5 4 3 2 1

CHAPTER

1

Martin Chezzlewit was eighty-five years old and not in the best of health. At times his mind was clear as a bell, but there were times when he made no sense at all. He'd been a butler at the Manor House for more than sixty years, long before the Earl of Wellsborough's daughter, Lady Elizabeth Hartleigh Compton, was born.

Martin took his job quite seriously, but these days, what with the constant climbing of stairs, and the ever-present hazards of wartime England, his duties often became too much for him, and he would wander off to his room for a lengthy nap.

Therefore, when he failed to turn up at the appointed time for the midday meal that fateful day, at first no one was particularly concerned.

Violet, busy at the stove as usual, did her best to mangle whatever provisions could be scrounged from the measly offerings of rationed food. Cooking in wartime

England was a challenge for the best of cooks. Violet was not the best of cooks.

Elizabeth sat at the large kitchen table that had been scrubbed smooth by generations of housemaids, and anxiously scanned the newspaper for the latest accounts of the Allied invasion, which had occurred three days earlier. She had a personal interest in the events of the past three days. American flying officers billeted in her mansion had been involved in the battle.

Major Earl Monroe and his men had been absent from the Manor House for more than two weeks. Elizabeth was concerned for all the men, of course. Her concern for the handsome major, however, bordered on terror. News of the dangers faced by the pilots and their crews was sparse, but one didn't need an overactive imagination to understand the consequences of flying over occupied France and Germany.

Her calls to the American base had been met with polite but firm reminders that information to the general public was restricted. Since she could hardly reveal the fact that she was madly in love with the major and therefore could hardly be considered general public, she was forced to bite her tongue and go back to the interminable waiting that so many British women endured these days.

If only Earl were not in the middle of a lengthy divorce, if only she were not the lady of the manor and expected to conduct herself with decorum, if only this damn war would finally end and put everyone out of their misery, life would once more be bearable.

Wallowing in her own personal hell, she was unaware of Violet addressing her until she heard her name spoken much too sharply by her housekeeper.

"Lizzie! For goodness' sake, have you gone deaf?"

Elizabeth raised her head and frowned at Violet, who stood with her head tilted to one side, looking like an angry robin defending its nest. "I beg your pardon?"

"I've spoken to you three times, and you haven't heard a blinking word I said."

That was no excuse to talk to her in that manner, Elizabeth thought wryly, but then Violet had special privileges, thanks to her lifelong tenure at the manor and the fact that she and Martin were all that were left of the hordes of servants that once ran the Manor House so efficiently. "I'm sorry," she said, mustering up a smile. "I was thinking about something else. What did you say?"

Violet still looked put out. "I said, the rag and bone man came again today. I gave him those old curtains we pulled down last year. They almost fell to bits when I shook them out but he seemed pleased with them."

"That's nice," Elizabeth murmured.

"And stop worrying about the major." Violet withdrew a pie dish from the oven and slapped the door shut with a bang. "He'll be back soon enough."

Annoyed that her thoughts were so transparent, Elizabeth said stiffly, "I wish I had your optimism, not to mention your clairvoyance."

Violet clicked her tongue and turned to face her again. "You're going to worry yourself into an early grave, Lizzie. Why don't you—" She broke off as the door burst open and a pair of giggling girls tumbled into the kitchen.

Sadie was in the lead, and the boisterous housemaid came to a sharp stop when she caught sight of Elizabeth at the table. Polly, Elizabeth's young assistant, bumped into Sadie, sending her forward a step or two.

"How many times," Violet screeched, "have I told you two to watch your manners in Madam's presence!"

Both girls mumbled an apology and slid onto their seats at the table. "So who's going to an early grave, then?" Sadie demanded, having apparently overheard Violet's last remark.

The housekeeper ignored her and started dishing up the pie onto plates.

"No one, I hope," Elizabeth said, with a silent prayer. She looked at Sadie, wondering how to phrase the question uppermost in her mind. "I don't suppose you've heard from Joe?" she asked at last.

Sadie shook her head and reached for a plate of thinly sliced bread. "Not since the invasion, m'm. Don't suppose they can say much, though, can they. Especially since Joe is only my boyfriend. I'll say one thing for these Yanks, they know how to keep their mouths shut, that's for sure."

"Not like some people I could mention," Violet snapped, as she slapped a plate in front of Elizabeth.

She put the other plate down in front of Sadie, who looked at the pile of mashed potatoes covering a gray mess that defied description.

"What's this, then?" Sadie demanded, sniffing warily at the offering. "It doesn't look like shepherd's pie."

"Well, it is." Violet stomped back to the stove to get two more plates. "It's just a wartime version of it, that's all. It's Lord Woolton pie."

"What the flipping heck is that?" Sadie handed the plate of bread to Elizabeth, who took a slice, silently echoing Sadie's sentiments. The pie did look awfully dismal.

"It's a recipe Lord Woolton sent out. Everyone's using it nowadays." Violet returned to the table and placed a plate in front of Polly, and set another plate in front of Martin's empty chair.

"So who's he when his mother's home?" Sadie asked rudely.

Polly, who wore much the same expression as Sadie's when she observed her plate, piped up. "He's the Minister of Food, isn't he, m'm?"

"He is indeed," Elizabeth said. She couldn't help wondering what a member of the House of Lords knew about wartime recipes. Knowing the others wouldn't start before her, she picked up her fork and poked at the gooey mixture. "This does look rather odd, Violet," she said reluctantly.

"That's because there's no meat in it," Violet said crossly. She thumped a full boat of dark brown gravy down on the table. "Here, put some of this on it. It will make it taste better."

"Nothing's going to make this taste better," Sadie muttered. "Whoever heard of a shepherd's pie without meat?"

"We used up all our meat rations this week," Violet said, ignoring Sadie and addressing Elizabeth instead. "They all went on the steaks you wanted me to buy."

Elizabeth sighed. "I know. That was awfully extravagant, I must admit. But I did so miss Earl's steaks from the base."

"The steaks were very nice," Polly said helpfully.

Violet scowled. "Just thank your lucky stars you have an employer as generous as Lady Elizabeth. It isn't often an assistant gets to have her meals free."

"Polly's more than an assistant, Violet," Elizabeth said quietly, "as you well know. She's always welcome to eat here with us."

Polly nodded in relief. "I do appreciate it, m'm. Now that me mum's working nights in the canteen, she gets her meals there. I'm not much of a cook and I hate being in that house all by myself. It's so creepy."

"It must be hard for your mother, traveling back and forth to North Horsham every day," Elizabeth said, putting off the moment when she actually had to taste the pie.

"You can take that look off your face, young lady." Violet leaned over Sadie, dropped her own plate on the table, and sat down. "It's not going to poison you."

"What's in it, then?" Sadie demanded.

"Everything that's good for you." Violet picked up her knife and fork. "Potatoes, carrots, onions . . ."

"But no meat," Sadie said with disgust. "Why is it so sticky?"

"That's the oatmeal," Violet said, her voice rising. "Just eat it, will you, and stop complaining."

"Where's Martin?" Elizabeth asked, more to defuse the tension than anything. "He's not usually this late for his midday meal."

Violet shook her head at the empty chair. "Taking one of his long naps, I suppose. I'll put his plate in the oven to keep warm." She got up from the table again and shoved the plate into the oven. Everyone winced when she slammed the door shut.

"Are you going to watch them pull down the factory tomorrow, m'm?" Sadie asked. She took a mouthful of the pie, wrinkling her nose as she tried to get it down.

"Lots of people are going up there to watch," Polly chimed in.

"Well, neither of you will be there," Violet said, coming back to the table. "You've both got work to do.

Though I must say, I'll be glad to be rid of that eyesore. It looked so ugly after half of it burned down. It'll be lovely to have the rest of it gone now."

"They say they're going to use a big ball and chain to knock it down," Sadie said, her words muffled by the bread she was chewing.

"Don't speak with your mouth full," Violet snapped. "Finish your meal then go out there and get that washing in. It looks like rain this afternoon."

Apparently glad of the excuse to leave the rest of her pie, Sadie jumped up. "Excuse me, m'm. I'll go and get the washing now."

Elizabeth nodded, her mouth occupied with dealing with the pie as best she could.

"The rag and bone man says he's coming back next week." Violet picked up her knife and fork and tackled the unappetizing food on her plate. "I was wondering what else we had to give him. I feel sorry for him, I do. He seems so down and out, and that patch over his eye makes him look even worse. Lost his eye in the war, he did, poor devil. Must be horrible to only see out of one eye."

"He looks like a pirate," Polly said, pushing her plate away from her. "Acts like one, too, carting off everybody's stuff. What does he do with all that rubbish, I'd like to know?"

"Sells it, of course." Violet's expression changed as she swallowed some of her pie. She reached for the gravy boat and poured a generous amount over the offending mess on her plate. "That's what rag and bone men do. They collect stuff that nobody wants and they sell it to someone who does want it. You'd be surprised what some people will pay for stuff other people throw out. Especially from the Manor House."

"Well," Elizabeth murmured, giving up her valiant attempt to enjoy the meal, "perhaps we should think of selling it ourselves instead of giving it away. The roof needs repairs again, and if we don't do something about those noisy water pipes soon, nobody in the east wing is going to get any sleep."

Violet sniffed. "Since the only people who sleep in the east wing are the American officers, and we haven't seen hide nor hair of any of them for two weeks, I'd say that's the least of our worries right now."

"They'll be coming back any day now," Elizabeth said quietly. "All of them."

Something in her tone must have warned Violet, as she looked up, saying quickly, "Well, of course, I know that. I just meant for now, that's all."

The back door flew open just then, banging against the stove, as it was apt to do when opened too wide. Sadie struggled in, bearing a large basket full of clean, dry laundry. "You'll never guess what," she said breathlessly, as she dumped the basket in the middle of the floor. "All the bloomin' knickers are gone!"

Her statement was met with a disapproving frown from Violet, while Polly giggled behind her hand.

Elizabeth stared at Sadie, whose face was flushed with indignation. "I beg your pardon?"

"Sorry, mum. I meant the ladies' drawers. They're all *gorn*!"

Violet tutted. "Don't be ridiculous, Sadie. Undergarments simply don't just disappear. You probably didn't peg them firmly enough and the wind took them off the line."

Sadie scowled at her. "Then where are they, I'd like

to know? They'd be all over the back garden if they blew off, wouldn't they?"

"Oh, dear." Elizabeth stared at the basket. "Are you sure, Sadie? How many pairs are missing?"

"Well, I had three pairs out there, and Violet's long drawers were out there and your knickers were out there, too, m'm—"

She broke off as Violet gasped and rose to her feet. "Sadie Buttons, how dare you discuss Madam's unmentionables!"

"Well, she asked me," Sadie wailed.

"Violet, do sit down." Elizabeth smiled at Sadie. "It's all right, Sadie. Sit down and get your breath. You sound as if you've been running all the way up the hill."

"It's the shock, m'm." Sadie sank onto her chair. "I can't think why someone would want to steal all the knick—er, unmentionables."

"Probably that Clyde Morgan," Violet muttered. "I knew there was something fishy about him."

Elizabeth stared at her. "Clyde who?"

"Morgan. The rag and bone man." Violet shook her head. "I left him in here while I went to get the curtains. I bet he stole the . . . undergarments while I was upstairs."

Sadie made a sound of disgust. "Now who the heck would buy someone else's knickers?"

"Eeew," Polly said, screwing up her face. "I wouldn't, even if they was washed."

Elizabeth sighed. "Well, I don't suppose there's much we can do about it. We can hardly go around the village asking everyone if they bought ladies' drawers from the rag and bone man."

Polly giggled again, earning a scowl from Violet.

"I'm just glad Martin isn't sitting here listening to all this," Violet muttered.

"He'd probably have a flipping heart attack," Sadie said, her grin suggesting she'd recovered from her shock.

Elizabeth glanced up at the clock on the mantelpiece. "He is awfully late, Violet. Do you suppose he's all right?"

Violet grunted and got to her feet. "He's probably snoring away in his bed and dreaming he's twenty again. I'll take him a cup of tea. The kettle should be boiling by now. Meanwhile, Sadie, sort out that washing and fold it. You can get the ironing done this afternoon." She got up from the table and went over to the stove for the teakettle.

Sadie left the table to sort the laundry, and Polly pushed her chair back, too. "I'd better get back to the office, m'm," she said. "I've got some letters to sort out."

Elizabeth nodded. "Very well. How is your penfriend project working out these days?"

Polly and Sadie exchanged pleased glances. "We're getting lots of letters off to the boys abroad, m'm," Polly said proudly. "Nearly all the women in the village are writing to someone over there. Marlene says the boys are ever so pleased to get the letters."

"I'm sure they are." Elizabeth smiled. "You and Sadie are doing something very worthwhile for the war effort. Keep it up. How is your sister? Is she keeping well?"

Polly nodded eagerly. "Marlene says as how she might be coming home soon. They're sending a lot of the ambulance drivers home from Italy, though she may have to go to France next. I just hope she can stay here for a while. I really miss her, and I know Ma does, too."

"Well, give Marlene my regards when you write to her. Tell her I miss her, too. She always did such a beautiful job with my hair."

Polly's smile faded. "I don't know if she'll ever go back to being a hairdresser, m'm. She says as how the war has changed her, and she's talking about becoming a nurse when it's over."

"How splendid!" Elizabeth exclaimed. "We could certainly use dedicated people like her."

"Yes, m'm. I'll tell her you said so." Polly hurried out, and Elizabeth looked at Violet, who was pouring hot tea into the china teacups.

"It's very refreshing to see young people getting involved like this," Elizabeth said.

Violet carried a steaming cup and saucer over to Elizabeth and placed it in front of her. "About time they did something," she muttered. "Instead of nattering about film stars and clothes all the time."

Elizabeth glanced at Sadie, who rolled her eyes but, thankfully, held her tongue.

"Don't disturb Martin if he's sleeping," Elizabeth said, turning back to Violet. "He's seemed rather preoccupied lately. I hope he's not falling ill."

"The only thing wrong with Martin is his mind," Violet said crisply as she carried the cup and saucer over to the door. "If he didn't spend so much time talking to imaginary ghosts and worrying all the time about Germans invading us, he wouldn't get so worn out."

The door swung to behind her, leaving Elizabeth alone with Sadie, who was still occupied with sorting out the laundry.

"The thing that really makes me cross, m'm," Sadie muttered, "is that now I have to buy new knickers. I was saving up my coupons to buy a new blouse. Now I'll have to wait another two months."

"I might be able to spare a coupon or two," Elizabeth offered.

Sadie's face brightened considerably. "Oh, could you, m'm? That would be smashing. Really. I could pay you back later, if you like."

"There's no need for that." Elizabeth got up from her chair and fetched her handbag from the dresser. Opening it, she peered inside, then fished out her coupon book. "Here." She tore out three coupons. "You may use these."

Sadie took them with a gasp of pleasure. "That's really good of you, m'm. Thank you ever so much."

Elizabeth smiled. "I can't have my housemaid running around without undergarments, now, can I?"

Sadie slapped a hand over a grin, just as the kitchen door burst open once more.

Violet stood in the doorway, still holding the cup and saucer. "He's not there," she said flatly. "Martin's not in his room. He seems to have disappeared."

CHAPTER

❈ 2 ❈

"Oh, dear," Elizabeth murmured. "I do hope Martin hasn't got himself lost again."

Violet stomped over to the sink and poured the tea into the drain. "Now we'll have to waste time looking for him, the silly old goat. Sadie, you look upstairs, I'll look down. If you don't find him up there, get Desmond to help you search the grounds."

"Don't bother Desmond," Elizabeth said, heading for the door. "I'll take the dogs and look for him outside. I could use some fresh air." She whistled to the burly animals dozing under the table. "Come, Gracie, come, George. Walkies?"

Both dogs leapt to their feet, nearly knocking over the table in their haste to get outside.

Violet shook her head. "They'll be more hindrance than help. They'll get the scent of a rabbit and they'll be off. You'll be spending more time looking for them than you will Martin."

Elizabeth opened the door and let the eager dogs charge into the hallway. "They're supposed to be part bloodhound," she said, pausing in the doorway. "I'll give them Martin's scarf to sniff."

"Just mind they don't eat it," Violet muttered. She turned on Sadie. "Go on, girl, start looking for that old fool. He's probably up in the great hall talking to the suit of armor again."

Sadie hurried out of the kitchen, stopping to pat the boisterous dogs on her way out. Elizabeth followed her, with Violet hot on her heels. They all parted company in the upstairs hallway, and Elizabeth let out a sigh of relief when she was out in the open air beneath a sky dotted with fluffy white clouds.

Tasting freedom, the dogs yelped and barked as they bounded across the courtyard, heading for the soft grass of the expansive lawns. Elizabeth watched them, smiling at their antics.

Remembering the day Earl presented her with the wriggling puppies, a wave of longing swept over her. So many times she had waited, her heart full of dread, for him to come safely back to the manor. Each time he'd returned, she'd sent up a prayer of thanks, knowing that the next good-bye could be the last.

These days the waiting seemed to get harder each time he left, and never as agonizing as it was right now. With news of the invasion filtering through in dribs and drabs, she knew only that the Allied forces, though making some headway, were taking heavy losses.

According to the latest news, they had secured beaches and were building artificial harbors for the landing operations, with the help of Allied bombing raids on the enemy lines.

It was this last part that concerned her the most, of course. Earl was in the midst of it all, flying through those perilous skies with nothing between him and the flying bullets but a sheet of thin metal.

Just the thought of it filled her veins with ice. This had to be his most dangerous mission so far. He'd been fortunate up until now. He'd even been shot down once and returned with little more than a limp and a plaster on his forehead.

How long could his luck hold out? She'd heard the men talking, saying the more missions they flew, the greater the odds against them coming back.

The dogs barked, chasing away her morbid thoughts. They stood side by side several yards off, impatient to go to the cliffs, where they could race and tumble in the deep grass.

First, she reminded herself, they had to at least make a token effort to look for Martin. She headed toward the dogs, waving Martin's scarf and wondering what on earth had possessed her to imagine they could actually understand what she wanted from them.

It was more than two hours later when she finally returned to the manor. By then, exhausted and hungry, she'd forgotten her original mission. She'd allowed the dogs to romp until they were ready to drop, while she'd indulged in her favorite pastime—reliving memories of all her meetings with Earl.

It wasn't until Violet dragged the heavy oak door open and Elizabeth caught sight of her housekeeper's face, that she remembered. "What happened?" she demanded, stepping inside. "Is Martin all right?"

"I don't know." Violet closed the door, then leaned against it for a moment before turning around. "He's still missing. The girls and I have searched everywhere in the manor. Desmond has searched the grounds. He even bicycled down to the village, in case Martin had taken it into his head to walk down there. Though, slow as he walks, he would never have got that far until after dark. There was no sign of him." She shook her head. "I don't know where he's gone, Lizzie. He's missed his meal and it's almost time for supper. He's never done that before. I have to tell you, I'm really worried. I'm afraid something terrible might have happened to him this time. What are we going to do?"

By the time the long summer twilight finally gave way to dusky night, Martin still hadn't returned to the Manor House. Just to be sure, Violet sent Polly and Sadie on another extensive hunt throughout the mansion, until everyone was convinced the elderly gentleman was not inside.

Greatly worried, Elizabeth rang the police constable at home, since the police station had closed its doors several hours ago. Judging by P.C. George Dalrymple's tone, he'd been woken up from a deep sleep, for which Elizabeth profusely apologized.

"You know I wouldn't disturb you if I wasn't certain these are dire circumstances," she assured him, after she'd recounted all the efforts they'd made to find Martin. "I'm afraid he's wandering around in the woods somewhere, though why he would be there in the first place I can't imagine."

"Well, you know the old boy's a bit dotty, your ladyship," George said, still sounding irritable. "I'm just surprised he hasn't wandered off before this. He'll turn up in the morning as bold as brass, you'll see."

"No one," Elizabeth said with emphasis, "is going to get any sleep while Martin is out there somewhere in the dark, alone and probably lost and confused. It's damp out there at night. He could get pneumonia and at his age that could very well be the death of him."

Standing behind her in the kitchen, Violet clicked her tongue in dismay. Ignoring the interruption, Elizabeth said firmly, "I waited until I was certain Martin was officially missing. I must insist that we send out a search party immediately. My staff and I will search the woods adjoining the estate. I suggest you round up as many volunteers as you can find and organize them to search the rest of the area."

George's resigned voice echoed wearily down the line. "Very well, your ladyship. I'll see what I can do."

"Right away, George."

"Yes, m'm. Right away it is."

Elizabeth hung up the phone, trying to feel reassured. Violet sat at the table, her arms crossed over her flat chest. Huddled in front of the stove, Polly's and Sadie's faces were strained with worry.

"I know it's late," Elizabeth said, appealing hopefully to the girls, "and I wouldn't ask if I didn't think—"

"It's all right, m'm," Sadie butted in. "Me and Polly would love to help look for him, wouldn't we, Pol?"

"'Course we will, m'm. I couldn't sleep not knowing what had happened to Martin."

"Me neither," Sadie declared. "He's a funny old bloke and he's got a screw or two missing and I know he calls me names and everything but I know he'd do the same for me if it was the other way around."

Elizabeth seriously doubted that, but she nodded in agreement anyway. "Good. I'm going to take the motorcycle and search the lanes. I wonder if you two wouldn't mind searching the woods?"

Polly looked scared but she lifted her chin and linked her arm through Sadie's. "If Martin is in the woods, we'll find him," she said stoutly.

"We'll take torches with us," Sadie added.

Polly gasped. "What about the blackout?"

"Nobody'll see the lights in the woods, silly. Besides, it's getting on for midnight. Who's going to be walking around this late at night?"

"Just be careful," Elizabeth told them. "I don't want you two getting into any trouble."

"You can't ride that motorcycle in the dark," Violet said. "Without lights you won't see a thing."

"There's enough moonlight for me to see the road," Elizabeth assured her.

Violet got to her feet. "I'm coming with you. You'll need your eyes to watch the road. I can watch out for any sign of Martin."

Elizabeth regarded her warily. "You'd have to ride in the sidecar."

Violet flinched, but reached for the maroon knitted cardigan she always left hanging behind the door. "While we're standing around talking about it, we could be out there looking."

"Come on, Pol," Sadie said, dragging Polly to the door. "Let's get cracking. The sooner we find him the sooner we can get to bed." They disappeared into the hallway, earning Elizabeth's heartfelt gratitude.

A few minutes later she and Violet were on their way down the shadowy driveway, crawling along at a snail's pace to peer into the trees that lined the long, winding path. Turning into the lane, Elizabeth sent up yet another silent prayer. First Earl, now Martin. *Please, please, let them at least find one of them safe and sound.*

For two hours they crawled down lanes and byways, stopping every now and then to peer over gates and hedges, circling the village twice before finally having to admit defeat. Hampered by the darkness, it was impossible to see farther than a few yards in the dense undergrowth that lined the fields and downs, and even Violet, who never gave up on anything, suggested they get some sleep and continue the search in the morning.

In a last desperate measure, Elizabeth pulled up on the coast road and cut the engine. "If we both yell together," she told Violet, "Martin might hear us and call out. Our voices will carry from up here. If he's in the woods, maybe the girls will hear him."

"If they're still out here," Violet grumbled. "It's got to be long after midnight."

"It's worth a try." Elizabeth climbed off the saddle and went to the edge of the road. Facing the woods, she put both hands to her mouth. "On three," she said. "Both together. One, two, three . . . *Martin!*"

Their combined voices echoed across the downs, then faded away. The only sound that answered them was a scuffling in the deep grass a few yards away, and the steady clip-clop of a horse's hooves off in the distance.

"One more time," Elizabeth said, cupping her mouth once more. "One, two, three . . . *Martin!*"

Violet's voice cracked on the shout, and Elizabeth's throat felt raw with the effort of shrieking her butler's name. "All right," she said wearily. "I suppose we shall have to just wait until daylight and look for him then."

"Let's just hope he has enough sense to find somewhere warm to sleep," Violet muttered.

Elizabeth climbed back on the motorcycle, knowing full well that neither of them would sleep comfortably in their beds knowing Martin was out there somewhere in the cold, damp black of night, alone and more than likely feeling abandoned.

Sadie was already asleep in her room when they got back to the Manor House. Violet went to peek in Martin's room just in case he'd returned, but she came back to the kitchen with a long face that dashed Elizabeth's hopes.

As she expected, Elizabeth tossed and turned the rest of the night, slipping in and out of sleep until the twittering sparrows finally got her out of bed at the break of dawn. All night long she'd listened for the shrill ring of the telephone, not really sure if she was waiting to hear about Martin, or if her thoughts were more concerned with the long silence from Earl.

Much to her surprise, Violet was already up and pottering about the kitchen when Elizabeth entered it some time later. It was not yet six o'clock, but the sun streamed through the windows and bathed the kitchen in a warm glow.

While her housekeeper poured her a steaming cup of tea, Elizabeth rang George's house again. This time his wife answered.

"He's gone down to the station early, your ladyship," Millie said. "He's really worried about poor Mr. Chezzlewit. We were all out looking for him last night until it got too dark to see."

"I appreciate all your efforts," Elizabeth said, feeling ridiculously close to tears. "I just can't think where he could be."

"I'm sure he's all right, m'm. My George will find him today, I'm sure."

Wishing she could feel as confident, Elizabeth hung up the telephone. "I'm going down to the police station," she told Violet. "I just can't sit around here not knowing what they are doing about this."

"Breakfast first," Violet said. "You need something in your tummy before you go out."

"I'm too upset to eat." The morning newspaper lay on the table and she picked it up. "I don't suppose there's any more news about the invasion."

"Haven't had time to read it yet." Violet stirred a simmering pot of porridge with a large wooden spoon. "More doom and gloom in there, no doubt."

Elizabeth scanned the headlines. "It's not much different from yesterday's news. I wish they would tell us what's really going on over there."

"So it could worry you all the more, I suppose." Violet spooned the thick, gooey porridge into a bowl. "Here, get this down you. You'll feel better for it."

Elizabeth obediently sat, her glance straying to Martin's empty chair. "Poor Martin. I'm afraid he's in real trouble this time."

Violet turned away so sharply Elizabeth suspected she had tears in her eyes. "Silly old goat. What did he have to go out on his own for? You'd think he'd know better."

"Probably looking for Germans," Elizabeth murmured. "I hope he didn't take that old blunderbuss with him."

"No, it's still hanging on the wall. Besides, it's so old he'd never get it to fire."

"That's what we thought that night he fired it at Earl." Elizabeth smiled. "Do you remember that night? He thought Earl was attacking me and he shot at him with the blunderbuss."

Still with her back turned, Violet's shoulders shook. "Knocked him off his feet it did, silly old fool. Good job there weren't no bullets in that thing. He'd have blown the major's head right off."

Remembering how Earl had thrown her to the floor and protected her with his body, Elizabeth's smile faded. Surely, *surely,* she wasn't going to lose both of them at the same time. That would be just too much to bear.

It didn't help when an odd sound escaped from Violet, which Elizabeth could swear was a sob. She busied herself with pouring the cream from the top of the milk bottle onto her porridge in order to give her housekeeper time to compose herself.

When she thought it was safe to talk again, Elizabeth said lightly, "Well, it looks as if it will be a good day to pull down that dreadful factory. At least it's not raining, and the wind seems fairly light."

"Good thing to be rid of that." Violet's voice was muffled, as if she had a bad cold.

Elizabeth ate her porridge as fast as her strict upbringing allowed, then pushed her chair back and stood. "I'm going to run down to the station," she said to Violet's back. "Is there anything you need?"

"No, thanks, Lizzie. I'll be going to the shops myself later. You just try to find that old fool, all right?"

"I'll certainly give it my best effort." Elizabeth left the kitchen and hurried up the steps to the front door. Stopping just long enough to grab her coat from the hall stand and the silk scarf to tie around her hair, she let herself out into the cool morning air.

A cloudless blue sky confirmed her estimate of a nice day, and as she wheeled her motorcycle out of the stable she prayed that the rain would stay away until

Martin was found. She refused to contemplate the possibility that it might already be too late to save her butler. The Manor House without Martin was simply too bleak to visualize.

On the outskirts of the village, the demolition team had already assembled in front of the burned-out ruins of the munitions factory. The workmen, mostly elderly or physically impaired in some way, stood around drinking hot tea from their thermos flasks and munching on slabs of bread pudding, while grumbling about the long ride from North Horsham.

A stray dog, hungry for food, circled them warily, waiting for a morsel that could be snapped up before it dropped to the ground.

The foreman, a muscular ginger-haired brute, strode around issuing orders to which no one paid attention. Only one man appeared to be working and that was the driver of the crane that carried the wrecking ball.

As the huge machine lumbered across the uneven ground, the men moved out of its way, but otherwise paid little attention to it. Their job would start once the remains of the building fell in a heap of dust and broken bricks. What had once been a promising enterprise, supplying much-needed arms and ammunition to the troops fighting abroad, would be reduced to rubble in a matter of minutes.

The first thunderous crash of the wrecking ball shook the ground, and some of the men turned their heads to watch the destruction. Again and again the ball struck, startling the crows and causing a mass exodus from the nearby trees. Even the dog abandoned its hungry vigilance and slunk away.

Dust rose in an ugly cloud above the forlorn ruins as the crane backed away, its morbid job completed. The men reluctantly put away their flasks and prepared to begin the massive cleanup.

As they moved toward the rubble the dog reappeared, darting ahead of them with its nose in the air as if chasing an enticing odor. It leapt over a pile of bricks and began scrabbling madly at a heap of mangled wood and plaster.

One of the men at the head of the group shouted, and bent to pick up a lump of plaster to throw at it. Then he paused, his arm in midair. The rest of the men crowded behind him, staring with disbelief at what the dog had uncovered.

The man in front shuddered, then said quietly, "I think we'd better get the bobbies up here quick."

Someone else called out, "Get that flipping dog off the poor bugger."

"Not that it matters now," the first man muttered. "That poor sod's a goner. Looks like someone's put a bullet right through his bloody head."

CHAPTER
3

Elizabeth arrived at the station just as Sid, George's intrepid partner, was leaving. He greeted her with his usual good humor, though she could tell he was a little put out about something.

"I take it George is inside?" she asked him, nodding at the small brick building that once housed horses and still bore the faint aroma of their presence.

"Yes, your ladyship, he is indeed," Sid said grimly.

Being well used to the feuding between the two constables, Elizabeth refrained from asking about the problem. Both men had been retired for several years when the outbreak of war and the need for younger men in His Majesty's Service had removed the entire police force from Sitting Marsh.

George and Sid had been more or less forced out of retirement to serve their country. Neither of them was too pleased about being deprived of his former pursuits and got by expending as little energy as possible on police business. Their resentment often spilled over into personal attacks on each other, which certainly didn't help the situation.

Nevertheless, there were certain procedures that had to be followed before Elizabeth could feel justified in taking matters into her own hands, which she often did, much to the outward annoyance and secret relief of George, who more often than not was completely out of his depth.

In this case, however, she would need the full cooperation of both men if she was going to launch the extensive search for Martin she had in mind. Upon learning that Sid was on his way to the bakery to pick up pastries for himself and George, she let him go on his way and entered the gloomy confines of the police station.

George sat behind his desk, the newspaper spread out in front of him. He seemed startled to see her and hastily folded the newspaper as he greeted her. "You're out and about early this morning, your ladyship. Has Martin turned up, then?"

"No, he hasn't." Without waiting to be invited, Elizabeth sat down on the visitor's chair. It was a particularly uncomfortable chair, and she never sat in it longer than she had to, which prompted her to come straight to the point. "I want to round up as many villagers as I can to help find Martin. I need you and Sid to help me do that as quickly as possible. The longer we delay, the worse off Martin will be when we find him."

George's expression frightened her. "We did a pretty thorough search last night, m'm. I don't know as if he'll be all that easy to find."

"Exactly, which is why—" She broke off with a start as the telephone on his desk jangled in her ear.

"Excuse me, your ladyship. I'd better get that." George reached for the telephone and stuck it against his ear. His voice turned pompous when he announced, "Sitting Marsh police station here. P.C. Dalrymple speaking."

He listened intently for a while, his expression gradually changing from slightly bored to interested to downright excited. "Very well," he said after a lengthy pause, "I'll be there right away. Don't touch anything until the doc and I get there." He replaced the receiver and ran a hand over his glistening bald head. "Well, I'll be blowed," he said softly.

Watching him, Elizabeth felt annoyed that whatever message he'd received had apparently taken his concentration away from the matter at hand. "George, about Martin—"

She was rather rudely interrupted by George's raised hand. "Begging your pardon, your ladyship, but a rather important matter has come up. I'm afraid the search for your butler will have to wait."

Bound and determined that nothing was going to stand in her way, Elizabeth leaned forward. "Nothing can possibly be as important as finding my butler quickly enough to prevent a tragedy."

George slowly got to his feet. "Well, m'm, I don't like to disagree with you, but I reckon a tragedy has already occurred. There's a dead body up at the munitions factory and I have to get up there right away before someone messes about with the evidence."

Shock froze Elizabeth to her chair and it was a moment or two before she could get the words out. "Who is it?"

George shrugged. "Don't know, your ladyship, do I. The men up there are from North Horsham so they wouldn't know if it was someone from the village. In any case, I shouldn't think it would be anyone from Sitting Marsh. After all, it's a couple of miles out there and who would want to be hanging around a burned-out building anyway? It's not like anyone's gone missing. . . ." His voice trailed off and his eyes widened as he stared at Elizabeth. "No," he said, violently shaking his head. "No, it couldn't be Martin. How would he get up there?"

Elizabeth shot to her feet so fast she almost lost her balance. "I'm going with you."

George held up his hand. "Now, now, your ladyship, you know I can't allow you to go poking around up there. Besides, it's probably some tramp got in there for shelter and passed away. Happens all the time, it does. I'll tell you soon enough if it's . . . if there's anything you should know."

He was talking to thin air, as Elizabeth had already charged out the door without waiting to hear what else he had to say. The roar of her motorcycle almost drowned out his next words when he reached her.

"Lady Elizabeth, I have to order you—"

"I'm going up there, George. You have no right to stop me and you know it."

Straining to be heard over the noise of the engine, George yelled, "I need to take a look before you go messing about up there!"

"Then stop screaming at me and get in the sidecar!" Elizabeth yelled back.

Just then Sid came rushing up to them, holding a paper bag bulging with Bessie's pastries. "What's the blinking fuss about?" he cried, waving the bag in the air.

"What's happened? Where are you going? You haven't had your grub yet."

George looked longingly at the bag, then back at Elizabeth. "Go and get my helmet, Sid," he ordered. "I'm going for a ride with her ladyship."

Seething with impatience, her heart sick with dread, Elizabeth waited for the constable to fit his bulky body into the sidecar.

Sid rushed out and thrust the helmet at his partner, who took it and crammed it on his head.

"If I don't come back," George told him grimly, "don't make a pig of yourself with them pastries. And read that note I left for you. It's important."

Sid had no time to answer as Elizabeth released the brake and they were off, careening up the street at a pace that brought a shout of protest tinged with fear from George.

She ignored him, intent on getting to the factory ruins as soon as possible. Part of her refused to believe that Martin could be lying dead up there. That was the part she clung to, despite the knowledge that the coincidence was troubling.

It seemed an eternity until they reached the demolition site. Having last seen the burned-out factory at close quarters, it seemed strange to Elizabeth to see nothing but piles of rubble lying where the building once stood.

There had been talk of rebuilding it, until public protests had persuaded the city council to abandon the idea. Personally Elizabeth applauded their decision, though she felt sad that the prospect of a richer economy had been so quickly destroyed. Sitting Marsh was losing its young people at an alarming rate. The factory might have kept some of them there, had it lived up to its promise.

She brought her motorcycle to a halt amidst curious stares from the small crowd of workers huddled together at one end of the crushed building. One of them apparently recognized her and there followed a chorus of greetings which she acknowledged with a graceful wave of her hand.

She climbed from her saddle and held the machine steady while George attempted to extract his body from the sidecar. Meanwhile one man detached himself and hurried toward her. She recognized the snow-white beard and sea captain's hat immediately.

"Good morning, Captain Carbunkle!" she called out as he approached. "I've been meaning to pay you and Priscilla a visit. I trust you enjoyed your honeymoon in the Highlands?"

The captain halted in front of her and swept off his cap with a little bow. "I did indeed, madam. I'm sure Prissy would enjoy telling you all about it." Cramming his cap back on his head, Carbunkle nodded at George, who was too busy struggling to escape the cramped innards of the sidecar to pay attention to him. Giving up, the captain turned back to Elizabeth. "Got a mess over there, I'd say. I just happened to stop by to watch them take the old wreck apart, seeing as how I was taking care of the place the night it blew up. Wanted to watch the old girl go down and pay my respects. I never expected something like this, though."

"Of course not," Elizabeth said, her gaze straying to the heap of rubble. "What a dreadful way to end such a noble endeavor."

In spite of the warmth of the June sun, Carbunkle

rubbed his hands together as if he were cold. "Must have been a shock for the crew, finding a stiff 'un like that."

"Did you recognize him?" Elizabeth asked quickly.

The captain shook his head. "They wouldn't let me get close enough. Thought I'd hang around a bit, though. Might get a look at him later on. Bit of excitement does the old heart good, you know." He turned to leave, then paused to add, "The little lady would be pleased to see you any time, your ladyship. I know she would."

"I'll drop by at the first opportunity," Elizabeth promised him, somewhat taken aback by his macabre enjoyment of the situation.

Turning her attention back to George, she found him still trying to extricate himself from her motorcycle. This took some considerable effort, and by the time he'd finally freed himself and straightened his helmet, the doctor's car had crept onto the site and parked alongside them.

Dr. Sheridan, the village physician and medical examiner for the local constabulary, doffed his hat and nodded at Elizabeth. Before she could return his greeting, George stepped in and announced his intention to observe the victim.

The two men marched over to the group of workers, who all began talking excitedly until George lifted his hand. "Just show us where the victim is," he barked.

One of the men stepped forward. "He's over here, mate. The dog dug him up and we had to chase it off. Looks a right mess, he does."

George beckoned to the doctor, and the two of them picked their way through the pile of bricks and plaster, while Elizabeth held her breath and prayed.

She watched the men bend over something at their

feet; then after a while the two of them straightened. They had a quick discussion, and the group of men observing the procedure murmured anxiously among themselves. Dr. Sheridan squatted down again, and George stumbled out of the debris and walked briskly back toward her.

She could tell nothing by his expression and she wrung her hands in agonizing anticipation. No matter what he told her, she had to be brave and maintain her composure, she reminded herself. The lady of the manor never displayed her emotions in public. She must remember that at all costs.

It seemed that everything around her had frozen into silence as she waited for George to speak. The group of men made no sound, all eyes on the crouched figure of the doctor. Even the birds were hushed, and only the crunch of George's boots broke the eerie stillness.

He came to a halt in front of her and cleared his throat. "It weren't Martin, your ladyship. Thank the good Lord."

She swallowed hard, biting back a cry of relief. "Thank you, George," she said when she could trust her voice again. "Who is it, then? Did you recognize the victim?"

"Yes, m'm, I did. It were Clyde Morgan."

The name sounded familiar, and she furrowed her brow. "I'm sorry, whom did you say?"

"The rag and bone man," George said, glancing back at the doctor, who was getting to his feet. "Poor devil. Doc says it looks like he done himself in."

Shocked, Elizabeth stared at him in dismay. She was about to ask him how the victim had died when George added, "Excuse me, your ladyship, but it seems the doc's finished so I'll need to have a word with him."

He started off to meet Dr. Sheridan, and Elizabeth

followed purposefully behind him. "I meant in private, m'm," he said, when she caught up with him. "This is police business."

"The victim is a resident of Sitting Marsh," Elizabeth said firmly. "That makes it my business, too."

Dr. Sheridan joined them just then, and apparently didn't have any qualms about divulging the results of his investigation. "Gunshot to the side of the head," he said, his voice clipped and professional. "Died instantly. The gun's still in his hand. I'm not an expert but it looks like a German pistol. Nasty business, that. Been dead at least twelve hours, poor blighter. Not a good way to go, all alone like that."

"Probably would never have known he were there if it hadn't been for that mutt digging him up," George said, with a bit more relish than Elizabeth felt necessary.

"What about his family?" she asked George. "They must be worrying about him, wondering where he is."

George nodded. "Got a wife and kids at home. I s'pose I'll have to get on down there and notify the widow." He looked hopefully at Elizabeth. "I do hate to do that job."

"I'll come with you if you like," she offered at once. "I don't know what comfort I can give the poor woman, but it might be a help to her to have another woman there."

"Good idea!" George looked at the motorcycle as if he wished it would blow up. "Why don't I meet you down there? The good doctor will give me a lift, I'm sure."

Dr. Sheridan appeared not to hear. He was staring at the ruined building with a frown of irritation. "Is that Carbunkle chap nosing around the body?" he barked, to no one in particular. "He's got no business doing that, pesky fellow." Still muttering to himself, he strode off toward the pile of wreckage, presumably to chase off Captain Carbunkle, who hovered over something that, thankfully, Elizabeth couldn't see from there.

Not that she was particularly squeamish. She'd had occasion to view more than one dead body since inheriting her position from her late father. On the other hand, if she could avoid staring at human remains, she greatly preferred to do so. Murder, or in this case suicide, was such a terrible waste of a life.

An acute pang of anxiety caused her to turn away from George. Although the dead man was not Martin, she still didn't know where he was, and then there was Earl, who, for all she knew, could be—No! She would not even entertain the thought.

"You all right there, m'm?" George inquired, sounding more curious than concerned.

"Quite." Elizabeth blinked hard and turned back to him. "The doctor could be occupied here for some time. He has to make arrangements for the body to be taken to the morgue, and I doubt that he'll want to go out of his way to give you a lift. So I suggest you stop behaving like a baby, George, and get back in the sidecar. We need to notify Mrs. Morgan before the village grapevine gets hold of the news."

Looking affronted by her sharp comments, George squeezed once more into the tiny compartment. "I don't think we need to be in quite such a hurry going back, your ladyship," he muttered. "There's that nasty curve going down the hill, and I don't like the feel of leaving the ground when you take the corners at breakneck speed like that."

Elizabeth pursed her lips. "I shall take your concern into consideration on the way back," she said stiffly.

"Thank you, m'm."

"Not at all, George." She stomped hard on the kick start and the engine roared to life. Sorely tempted to take off at top speed, she curbed her resentment and cruised from the site and out onto the road, doing her best to avoid the ruts and bumps.

Following George's directions, she sailed sedately down the hill into the village and pulled up in front of an untidy-looking house with a front garden that had been sadly neglected. Remnants of dying hollyhocks, limp dahlias, and forlorn daisies fought with each other for breathing space among the choking weeds, which had encroached upon the pathway and filled the cracks with gleeful profusion.

Picking her way up the path, Elizabeth cringed at the sight. Plants were living things, too, and deserved better. With George hovering behind her, she waited on the cluttered porch for someone to open the front door.

CHAPTER
❄ 4 ❄

When the door finally opened, the woman who stood there looked as if she'd just that moment fallen out of bed. The dressing gown she wore could have stood a good washing, her light brown hair hung in dismal strands around her face, and her eyes were red-rimmed and underlined with dark shadows. For a moment Elizabeth wondered if she'd already heard the news.

"Mrs. Morgan," she said gently, "we've come about your husband."

The woman stared at her as if she didn't understand the words, then she mumbled, "He's not here. I don't know where he is."

Feeling dreadfully sorry for the poor woman, Elizabeth put out a hand. "May we come in for a moment?"

Mrs. Morgan shot a hasty look at the room behind her. "The place's a mess," she said shortly. "I wasn't expecting visitors."

She'd made it sound like an accusation, and George

stepped forward. "Mrs. Morgan—Iris—this is Lady Elizabeth Hartleigh Compton, lady of the manor. It would be . . . polite to invite her inside."

Iris's eyes widened and she stepped back. "Oh, my. I'm so sorry, your ladyship. I didn't recognize you, I'm sure. You'll have to forgive the mess—"

"It's quite all right, Mrs. Morgan." Elizabeth stepped inside the narrow hallway, while words tumbled from Iris's mouth.

"I haven't been well, you see, and Clyde never came home last night, and I was up all night worrying about him. What with the kiddies home from school and everything, I haven't had time to tidy up, but if you'll just go in here . . ." She opened a door that led into a small parlor.

Standing in the doorway, Elizabeth gazed around the room in mute astonishment. Every inch of the walls was covered in an amazing array of knickknacks, from tiny portraits in antique frames and china dogs on decorative shelves to a huge Dig for Victory poster depicting a booted foot driving a garden spade into the soil. An enormous clock sat on the mantelpiece, ticking noisily away, its spidery hands pointing to large Roman numerals.

A cat leapt from the sofa and slunk behind an armchair as Elizabeth ventured farther into the room. The smell of boiled cabbage and stale cigarettes was almost overpowering and she held her breath for a moment as she paused in front of the sofa.

Iris chased the cat out and it jumped up on the chair. She shoved it off again, muttering, "I just washed that, you little bugger." The cat spat at her and stalked off, tail waving in the air behind it.

"Excuse my manners," Iris said, beckoning Elizabeth to sit down. "Let me get you a cup of tea."

"Please, don't bother yourself," Elizabeth said hastily.

"I'd like a cup of tea," George piped up. He sank onto a chair across the room, then, realizing Elizabeth hadn't yet sat down, sprang back to his feet.

Gingerly Elizabeth lowered herself onto the sofa, wondering how many cat hairs she'd have to get rid of before she could go anywhere near her dogs again.

Iris disappeared, and George, looking more comfortable than he had any right to be, took off his helmet and laid it in his lap. "You'll tell her, won't you, m'm?" he whispered.

Elizabeth was tempted to tell him it was his place to break the news, but knowing how clumsy George could be in these circumstances, she nodded her assurance.

While they waited, a child's voice could be heard in another room somewhere, singing loudly and out of tune. When Iris returned she carried a tray upon which she'd set a teapot, milk jug, sugar bowl, and three cups and saucers. There was also a small plate of broken biscuits, which she offered to Elizabeth, saying, "I'm sorry they're not whole biscuits, your ladyship, but these are the only ones I can get off ration. The kiddies eat the good ones as soon as I bring them home."

"Thank you," Elizabeth said, doing her best to control a shudder, "but I've just recently eaten breakfast."

George, it seemed, had no such qualms, and took a handful of the broken pieces, murmuring his thanks.

Elizabeth waited until the tea had been poured and served before saying quietly, "Mrs. Morgan, I'm afraid I have some very bad news."

Iris paused in the act of putting down the teapot and said carefully, "It's Clyde, isn't it. What's he done now?"

Elizabeth exchanged a quick glance with George. "He hasn't done anything, Mrs. Morgan. I deeply regret to have to tell you that your husband's body was found in the rubble of the munitions factory this morning. It appears he shot himself."

Iris's cry was pure agony. "Oh, my God, no."

"I'm so sorry." Elizabeth rose and put an awkward hand on the stricken woman's shoulder. "This must be a dreadful shock for you. Is there anyone we can contact to be with you?"

Shaking her head, Iris sank onto the nearest chair and buried her face in her hands. Her shoulders shook, while Elizabeth stood helplessly watching her, and George munched solemnly on his biscuits.

After a moment or two, Iris lifted her tearstained face. "I knew we would end up losing him one day," she said, wiping her nose with the back of her hand, "but I never thought it would happen like this."

George cleared his throat and fished a notepad out of his pocket. "Do you have any idea why Clyde would want to do away with himself?"

Iris shook her head. After a long pause, she said quietly, "He's been down in the dumps for a while 'cause business has been so bad. Nobody wants to get rid of anything these days. Everything's on ration, you see, and it's hard to buy new so everyone's hanging on to what they've already got."

She sniffed and dabbed at her nose again. "I just can't believe he's gone. I don't know what I'm going to do without him. Really I don't." She stared anxiously up at Elizabeth. "What's going to happen to my kiddies? They won't take them away from me, will they?"

"No one is going to take your children away from you," Elizabeth said firmly. "I'll see to that."

Iris wiped her eyes with her sleeve. "Thank you, m'm. I don't think I could go on if I lost them, too. They'll miss their father, that I do know." She nodded at a picture frame that stood on the sideboard.

The unkempt man in the photograph wore a straggly beard and a dark patch over his right eye. One hand was raised in the act of throwing a dart, and his thick brows were drawn together in concentration. He seemed rather formidable, Elizabeth thought, remembering Polly's comment about his resemblance to a pirate.

Feeling compelled to say something, she murmured, "He seems very . . . ah . . . capable. Was that taken at the Tudor Arms? I seem to recognize the bar behind him."

Iris nodded. "He's a good darts player, my Clyde." Her expression changed. "At least, he was." Her face crumpled, as if she were about to burst into tears again.

"As long as he wasn't drinking all night, that is," George said dryly.

Iris's chin shot up and her eyes filled with resentment as she glared at George. "That were an accident as you well know, George Dalrymple. And don't you never say otherwise."

Sensing an impending confrontation, Elizabeth said hurriedly, "Well, I must be off. I have to take George back to the station and then run some errands." She stared hard at George, who took the hint and stood, brushing crumbs from his trousers.

Jamming his helmet on his head, he said gruffly, "Well, I'm sorry about Clyde, Mrs. Morgan. I'm sure

Dr. Sheridan will be in touch with you shortly, and I'll ask the vicar to drop by to make arrangements for the funeral."

Iris slowly got to her feet, one hand hanging on to the armchair. She looked frail and helpless, and Elizabeth's heart went out to her.

"Is there someone who can take care of the children for a few days, just to give you some time to deal with all this?" she asked gently.

Iris shook her head. "No, your ladyship. But my Tommy's almost grown. Twelve years old, he is now. He'll help take care of Katie; she's only seven but she's no trouble. Thank you very much, m'm, but we'll manage."

"Very well." Elizabeth headed for the door, anxious now to breathe the fresh clean air outside. "But if you should change your mind, please let me know if there's anything I can do to help."

"You're very kind," Iris said, following them to the front door. She opened it for them and stood aside to let them pass. Just then the child's voice rang out, loud and surprisingly harsh. "Shut up, you sniv'ling little bugger, or I'll shut your mouth with *this*!"

Elizabeth raised her eyebrows at Iris, who shrugged her thin shoulders. "That's my Katie," she said, shaking her head. "Always bashing that poor teddy bear of hers. It's a wonder its head doesn't leave its shoulders, the way she carries on. Don't know what gets into her sometimes, really I don't."

Such language in a young child disturbed Elizabeth. She was even more upset that Iris apparently saw no reason to chastise the little girl for speaking in that dreadful manner. Such poor discipline would undoubtedly result in a problem child. It was none of her business, of course, and this certainly wasn't the time to bring up the subject. Instead, she merely nodded and followed George out into the welcome sunlight.

A few minutes later she pulled up outside the police station and cut the engine. George climbed grumbling and muttering out of the sidecar, and stretched his back with a loud moan.

Ignoring this rather childish display, Elizabeth demanded, "What about the search party? What's being done about finding Martin?"

"All taken care of," George said smugly. "I left a note for Sid. He should have half the village out looking by now. Unless they've found him already. If you'll hang on a minute, m'm, I'll go and see."

Seated astride the motorcycle, Elizabeth gripped the handlebars and silently prayed. George's voice interrupted her and she lifted her head.

"No one's there, your ladyship. No messages or anything, so I presume they are still out there looking for your butler."

"Very well. Thank you, George." She would have to be content with that for now, she thought dismally.

"Well, I'll be getting back to the desk then," George said. "I have to make up a report on Clyde Morgan."

Remembering the tension between Iris and George earlier, Elizabeth's curiosity got the better of her. "What did Iris mean about something being an accident?"

George frowned and scratched the back of his neck. "She was a bit touchy about that, weren't she? Can't say as I blame her. Nasty business that were."

He turned to leave, and Elizabeth shook her head. "George, I'd like to know what happened."

He paused, then turned back. "Oh, well, it were like this. A year or two ago Clyde was down the pub, drinking too much, like he always did. Anyway, they had a darts match and they was all betting on him to win it. There was this young girl, Sheila Redding, and she was watching the match. Only sixteen years old, she was. Clyde was fooling around and shot a wild dart. Buried it right in her head, he did."

Elizabeth uttered a shocked gasp. "Oh, good heavens. What happened to her?"

"Well, they got it out, but it did something to her brain. She's in a wheelchair, can't talk, or do much for herself. They put her in one of them homes for people like that. It's in North Horsham." George sighed. "Horrible thing to happen to someone that young. They say she'll never get any better."

"How awful." Elizabeth's heart ached for the girl. "Was Mr. Morgan charged with anything?"

"Not a thing. Iris were right about that. It were ruled an accident, though in my mind, he should have gone to prison for it. If he hadn't been drunk and fooling around, it would never have happened." George lifted his hand in a salute. "Thank you for the lift, m'm. Much obliged. Not my favorite way to travel by any means, but it's a lot faster than me bicycle, I will say that."

Elizabeth smiled. "I'll be quite happy to give you a lift anytime, George. You only have to ask."

He walked away from her, muttering under his breath. She couldn't swear to it, but it sounded as if he'd said, *Not on your bloody life.*

The wind had picked up when she rode up the hill, stinging her cheeks and bringing tears to her eyes. Normally she would be ravenously hungry by now, but her worries over Martin's absence and Earl's silence robbed her of an appetite.

Wearily she wheeled her motorcycle into the stables and walked around to the front door. She'd tugged on the bell rope several times before she remembered that Martin would not be there to open the door for her. Violet must not be able to hear the bell and Sadie in all likelihood was buried somewhere in the depths of the mansion. That meant she'd have to walk around to the back door of the kitchen.

She turned to go down the steps, then paused as the hollow sound of the bolts being drawn back echoed behind her. Violet must have heard the bell after all.

Waiting impatiently for the door to open, she decided to ring the hospital in North Horsham before going down to the kitchen for the midday meal. Someone might have found Martin and taken him there. Not that she had much hope of that, but it would give her something else to do besides waiting helplessly for news.

The door finally began to move, so slowly Elizabeth stared at it in alarm. Violet would have thrown it open, as would Sadie. Even Polly would not be inching it open in this furtive manner. Unless . . .

She put out a tentative hand and gently pushed. Feeling some resistance, she pushed harder, until a caustic voice spoke from the other side. "Hold on, hold on! What's the dashed hurry? I'm going as fast as I can!"

"Martin!" she screeched, and bounded forward without thinking. She heard a thud and a muffled yelp, and winced. Peering around the half-open door, she saw the elderly man leaning against the wall, one hand rubbing his forehead.

"Martin, I'm so terribly sorry. Are you hurt?"

"I'm not exactly basking in pleasure, madam." Very slowly he pushed himself away from the wall, righted his glasses, which had slipped down his nose, and smoothed back the half dozen hairs remaining on his head.

"Thank goodness, Martin. Wherever have you been? We've all been so dreadfully worried about you. We were quite sure something ghastly had happened to you. Are you hurt? Were you in an accident? Did you get lost? What on earth *happened* to you?"

Martin brushed imaginary dust from his trousers, then straightened as much as his bowed shoulders would allow. "I'm not at liberty to say, madam."

Taken aback, Elizabeth said tartly, "Martin Chezzlewit, you have been missing for an entire night. Half the village has been out searching for you—and still are, by all accounts. Violet and myself, as well as Sadie and Polly, were out until after midnight looking for you. You have worried us half to death and now you calmly say you can't tell me where you were or what you were doing?"

"That is correct, madam." He glanced across the hallway to the grandfather clock. "I do believe lunch is ready. Perhaps we should retire to the kitchen before Violet has a persnickety fit." He turned his back on her and began shuffling in his snail's-pace gait toward the kitchen steps.

Greatly annoyed, Elizabeth followed him. Having endured so much agony over the past twenty-four hours, she was determined to find out exactly what Martin was up to, and why he refused to talk about it.

Judging from the raised voices in the kitchen, Sadie and Polly had already arrived for their meals. Rather than wait for Martin to make the tedious climb down the stairs, Elizabeth passed him and reached the kitchen ahead of him.

She pushed open the door and the voices abruptly ceased. Violet busied herself at the stove, while Polly sat at the table with Sadie. Both girls jumped to their feet as Elizabeth entered.

She answered their greetings then turned to Violet, whose concentration was on the stew she was spooning onto the dinner plates. "Did Martin tell you where he was last night?"

Violet shook her head without turning around. "Don't talk to me about that old fool. Gone all night he was, and not a word as to where he's been. Won't say anything, except he's 'not at liberty to say.'"

She'd uttered the last words in a high-pitched voice that was supposed to mimic Martin's quavery one. Polly giggled, while Sadie's face seemed drawn and tense.

"Well," Elizabeth said, taking her seat at the table, "he will have to tell us sooner or later. He can't expect us to simply ignore his absence, when it caused so much fuss. What am I going to tell George, or the people who were out looking for him? Can you imagine what Rita Crumm will say when she finds out he's back and not a word about where he's been?"

Violet sniffed. "Rita Crumm would make a storm in a teacup about anything you did, as you well know. I wouldn't go worrying your head about her."

"Yeah, m'm," Polly said, reaching for a jagged slice of bread that looked as if it had been hacked off the loaf. "That Rita's jealous of you, that's all. Everybody knows that."

Elizabeth sighed. "I really don't know what she has to be jealous about. What with all the responsibilities of taking care of the estate and the tenants, and all the repairs that need doing to the manor, the dreadful crimes that have been committed in the village, and the incompetence of the constabulary . . ."

She paused for breath and Violet finished for her, "Not to mention a certain American major who hasn't been around lately."

That most of all, Elizabeth thought gloomily.

"Even with all that, m'm," Polly said, watching Violet carry two steaming plates to the table, "I reckon Rita Crumm would change places with you in a moment."

"That woman needs to be taken down a peg or two." Violet placed a plate in front of Elizabeth. "Just because she formed the Housewives League doesn't make her a blinking god. You'd think she was winning the war all by herself, to hear her talk. Makes me sick, she does."

"The Housewives League." Polly made a sound of disgust in her throat. "That lot cause more trouble than Hitler's bombs do. What with their watching for submarines and keeping guard on the cliffs with their pots and pans, hunting for spies, poking their noses into everything, and messing everything up."

"They've done good things, too," Elizabeth reminded her. "They've knitted woollies for the military, collected tinfoil, kept victory gardens, and held bazaars and fetes to raise money for planes and ammunition."

The door swung open just then and Martin crept in, sending everyone into silence. They all sat, staring at him expectantly, while he shuffled over to the table and took his seat.

Without a word Violet dished up some more stew and put it down in front of him. No one spoke as he lifted his knife and fork and began eating.

The silence seemed to stretch into hours, then for the first time since Elizabeth had sat down at the table, Sadie spoke, saying abruptly, "I haven't heard from Joe."

It was the last thing Elizabeth expected to hear, and Sadie's tone of voice warned her that the girl was as frantic about her boyfriend as she herself was about Earl.

Very carefully, she put down her knife and fork and dabbed at her mouth with her serviette. "With everything that's going on in France, I would be very surprised if we heard anything just yet. You know how secretive they have to be about everything."

Sadie avoided her gaze. "Yes, m'm. I suppose that's it."

Elizabeth's heart started thumping with apprehension. "I don't suppose . . ." Aware of Violet's sharp gaze, she let her voice trail off.

"No, m'm. I haven't heard nothing about no one."

Violet started talking just then, preventing Elizabeth from saying anything else. She sat quietly, eating her stew without tasting a single bite. All her thoughts and prayers were concentrated on Earl and his safe return. Right at that moment, that was all that mattered to her.

CHAPTER
❊ 5 ❊

Elizabeth spent the afternoon in the office catching up on the correspondence that seemed to have piled up over the past few days. With Polly's help she answered requests, complaints, and questions, juggled bills, and compiled the agenda for the next town council meeting.

Writing down Captain Carbunkle's name, she remembered her promise to call in on the newlyweds. First thing in the morning, she promised herself. It would help keep her mind off the problem of Earl and his whereabouts.

Violet was alone that evening when Elizabeth went down to the kitchen for supper. The moment she saw her housekeeper's face, she knew something was up. For a dreadful moment she thought Martin had gone missing again.

Especially when Violet hissed at her, "That silly old goat needs his head examined."

Elizabeth sat down heavily on the chair. "What now?"

Violet shook her head, waved a hand in the air, and appeared lost for words.

Alarmed, Elizabeth said sharply, "For heaven's sake, Violet. Spit it out. What is it?"

"It's Martin," Violet spluttered.

Having already guessed that, Elizabeth curled her fingers in frustration. "Is he missing again?"

"No, he's in his room. He'll be here any minute for his supper."

"Then you'd better hurry up and tell me what's got you in such a dither."

"I found a pair of knickers in his room."

Stunned, Elizabeth could only stare at her.

"I went in there this afternoon." Violet picked up a large butcher's knife from the kitchen counter and began furiously chopping a beetroot into thin slices. "The old fool refused to tell me where he'd been all night, and I thought there might be something in his room that would tell me."

Bloodred juice spurted across the chopping board and onto the floor. Ignoring it, Violet went on chopping. "Right there on his dresser. *Right there in the open*"— she smacked the knife down hard—"bold as brass, was a pair of my best drawers."

Elizabeth shut her mouth, swallowed, then said calmly, "I'm sure there's an explanation—"

"Oh, there's an explanation all right." Violet reached for another beetroot and began chopping again. "He's gone blinking bonkers, that's the explanation. He's the one been stealing the drawers off the line outside. I told you this would happen. I could see it coming a mile off."

She turned to face Elizabeth, the dripping knife held in her hand. "We have to get him out of the house. We have to put him in an asylum. We've got two young ladies to worry about. We can't have a demented old fool going around stealing their unmentionables. God knows what he'd get into next. I hate to think, honest I do."

Elizabeth sighed. "Calm down, Violet. I'm sure there's a perfectly good—"

She broke off as the door swung open and Martin appeared in the doorway. He took two steps into the kitchen, stopped, clutched his heart, and uttered an ear-piercing scream.

Elizabeth jumped, while Violet waved the knife at her. "See? What did I tell you? He's gone off his blinking rocker."

Martin stared at Violet with something akin to horror on his face, one hand still clutching his chest, his mouth opening and shutting with, mercifully, no more sound coming out of it.

Still shaken by the awful shriek, Elizabeth leapt to her feet. "It's his heart," she cried, rushing toward him. "He's having a heart attack."

Martin's faded blue eyes focused on her, and he shook his head. One trembling hand pointed at Violet. He whispered something, then coughed, and finally got some coherent words out. "Violet, madam. She's bleeding all over the floor."

"What?" Elizabeth spun around to look at her house-keeper.

Violet stood quite still, a dumbfounded expression on her face.

Elizabeth let out her breath in a puff of relief. "That's

not blood, Martin," she said, feeling a desperate urge to laugh. "It's beetroot juice. Look, Violet's cutting up beetroot."

"Oh, my God." Martin staggered over to his chair and leaned on the back of it, apparently too spent to make the effort to sit down. "I thought she'd cut off one of her blasted fingers."

"You silly old fool!" Violet brandished the knife at him, making Elizabeth quite nervous. "What were you doing with my knickers in your room? Tell me that!"

Elizabeth uttered a soft groan. She'd rather thought that they would tread around the matter with some delicacy. Blurting it out like that was not likely to encourage Martin to enlighten them.

To her immense surprise, Martin raised his head and in a voice that had regained considerable strength declared, "If you are referring to that offensive flannel undergarment on my dresser, you might want to explain how it ended up at the end of the driveway, in full view of anyone passing by."

It was Violet's turn to look astonished. "At the end of the driveway?"

"That's what I said." Martin turned to Elizabeth. "May I have your permission to join you at the table, madam?"

Trying desperately to keep a straight face, Elizabeth said solemnly, "Of course you may, Martin. Please sit down."

"Thank you, madam. I shall be honored."

"What do you mean, at the end of the driveway?" Violet demanded. "How did my . . . unmentionables get there?"

"Well, I shouldn't think they walked there all by

themselves." Martin's bones creaked and cracked as he settled himself on his chair.

Violet looked at Elizabeth, her cheeks pink with embarrassment. "I swear I don't know what he's talking about."

"Maybe the dogs took them down there," Elizabeth suggested.

"What, and unpinned them from the clothesline? Where's the rest of them, then?" Violet gave Martin a sharp glare. "You don't have any more hidden under your bed, by any chance?"

Martin looked offended. "Why, in heaven's name, would I hide your undergarments under my bed? In any case, if I were to indulge in such juvenile behavior, I would undoubtedly choose something infinitely more attractive than those hideous baggy bloomers you wear."

"Is that so?" Violet's eyes blazed with anger. "Like Polly's or Sadie's unmentionables, for instance?"

"Violet—," Elizabeth began, but Martin interrupted her.

"How dare you, madam!" He started to rise to his feet, struggled for a bit, then gave up and plopped back down. "I refuse to be insulted in this way."

"How do you know what I wear, anyhow?" Violet brandished the knife a little too close to his face for Elizabeth's comfort. "Have you been spying on me, you crazy old goat?"

"Your undergarments hang on the washing line in full view of everyone," Martin declared. "I keep expecting them to take off in the wind. It's really not surprising they ended up at the end of the driveway. With the wind in sails that large, I would expect them to reach China."

Deciding it was time to intervene, Elizabeth said

quickly, "Martin, just when and where did you find Violet's underwear?"

Martin gave her a reproachful look. "As I've already indicated, madam. I found them at the end of the driveway. They were just lying there, like—"

"Quite. When was that?"

"When I returned to the manor this morning, madam."

"Returned from where, Martin?"

She'd slipped the question in, hoping to catch him unawares. He was more alert than she'd anticipated. "I regret I'm not at liberty to say, madam."

"I'm not trying to pry into your personal affairs, Martin—," she began, but Violet interrupted.

"We have a right to know where you go, you old fool. We're responsible for you. What if something happened to you? How would we know where to find you?"

"I'm quite sure someone would alert Madam," Martin said, apparently unperturbed by Violet's outburst. "In any case, I was in no danger, I can assure you of that."

Giving up, Elizabeth shook her head at Violet, who seemed determined to pursue the matter. Martin would enlighten them when he was good and ready and not before. They just had to be patient, and trust that his assurances of his safety were valid.

"So you noticed the underwear on the driveway this morning?" she said, effectively silencing Violet.

"Yes, madam. I thought it prudent to pick them up, with some considerable distaste I might add, and return them to their owner. I visited my room first, and must have been distracted, since I forgot about them until now." He turned a watery gaze on Violet. "Had I foreseen the fuss such a valiant gesture would create, I would have left the repulsive garment where it was."

Elizabeth frowned. "But I left the manor before you returned, Martin. I didn't see anything lying in the driveway."

"Then it must have blown there after you left, madam."

"All the way to the driveway?" Violet demanded. "They would have to fly clear over the manor to do that."

"Unless," Elizabeth said slowly, "they were not the ones stolen yesterday. Did you put a new line of washing out on the line this morning, Violet?"

"Well, yes, I did. . . ." A look of alarm crossed Violet's face. "Oh, no, don't tell me—" She dropped the knife with a clatter on the table, spun around, and headed for the back door. "If they're gone as well I won't have any clean ones left." She dragged open the door and rushed outside.

Elizabeth held her breath, until an agonized shriek told her the worst.

Violet burst back through the door, her frizzy gray hair standing on end. *"Gone!"* she cried. "Every last blooming pair of them. Yours, too, Lizzie. Polly's and Sadie's as well. All gone. Now what are we going to do?"

Elizabeth puffed out her breath in exasperation. "It appears we have a thief on our hands. I shall have to let George know about this. Apart from the obvious inconvenience this person is causing, I don't like the idea that a lawbreaker is making a habit of trespassing on our premises. This could be quite a nuisance."

"I can't understand how the thief gets in and out without Desmond noticing." Violet waved her hands in agitation. "I know he's not much of a gardener, but he has two perfectly good eyes."

"I'll have a word with him," Elizabeth promised. "I'll warn him to keep a lookout."

"Might I suggest that if you'd let those abominable hounds of yours loose outside instead of mollycoddling them in the house all the time," Martin observed, "perhaps we wouldn't have to worry so much about trespassers."

"I'm afraid George and Gracie are much more likely to play with the intruder than chase him off." Elizabeth leaned down to pat the soft head of the nearest dog by her feet.

"Well, for once Martin's right. You do treat them like children." Violet turned back to the stove. "No wonder they're no good as guard dogs."

The dogs *were* her babies, Elizabeth thought fondly. Hers and Earl's. The closest she'd ever come to sharing a family with him. The thought of him brought a stab of anxiety. With each passing hour now she worried more about his safety. Never had he been absent this long without somehow getting word to her that he was safe. She was dreadfully afraid—She cut off the thought before it had time to form. There was no need to tempt fate. He would return to her. It was as simple as that.

The next morning Elizabeth awoke with a feeling of foreboding that would not go away, no matter how hard she tried to focus on other matters. After ringing George at the station and giving him an awkward report of the missing undergarments, she went down to the kitchen, where she found Polly and Sadie in an outrage at the loss of yet more of their precious clothes.

"Why would he take just the knickers?" Polly demanded, close to tears. "Why didn't he take all the other clothes?"

Elizabeth exchanged an uncomfortable glance with Violet, who immediately turned back to the stove.

"Because he's blooming batty," Sadie said. "A nutter. He belongs in the loony bin."

"Well, I suppose that might be a safer place for him than running around our grounds," Elizabeth agreed. "In the meantime, I want you girls to be extra careful. Don't go outside alone, and be on the watch for a stranger. He could be dangerous."

Polly looked scared, while Sadie seemed more furious than afraid. "Just let me get me flipping hands on him," she muttered. "I'll teach him to pinch me drawers."

"You'll do no such thing," Violet said briskly. "If you see someone stealing something like that you report him immediately to the constables."

"And by the time they got up here," Sadie said, nudging Polly, "he'd be long gone. I say we catch him ourselves and teach him a lesson."

Polly's face was drawn with anxiety, but she offered no resistance to Sadie's defiant statement.

"Sadie, I really don't think—" Elizabeth got no further, as just then the telephone shrilled, startling them all.

Violet reached for the receiver, while Elizabeth stood helpless, heart pounding, her leap of hope impossible to subdue. She watched her housekeeper speak into the telephone, then pause to listen, her head tilted to one side.

"I'll give her the message," she said at last, and hung up the telephone.

The disappointment was crushing, and Elizabeth struggled to keep her voice steady as she asked, "Who was that?"

"It was George." Violet glanced at the girls, then said quietly, "We're not the only one to lose our drawers. Seems quite a few women have had them stolen off the washing lines. George is worried. He thinks we have a lunatic loose in the village."

In spite of the warm sun sparkling on the ocean, the unsettling news, coupled with her worry over Earl, considerably dampened Elizabeth's spirits as she rode her motorcycle down to Sandhill Lane, where Wally Carbunkle lived with his new bride.

She missed Earl dreadfully. Even during the long months after he'd returned to America and she'd thought she'd never see him again, the aching misery hadn't felt this bad. Probably because at least she knew he was safe then, and there was always a glimmer of hope that he'd return. She had no such assurances now. In fact, the longer the silence, the more certain she became that something dreadful had happened to him.

Then again, there had been no word from any of the officers who'd billeted at the manor. They had obviously been confined to the base, a sure sign that their missions were even more dangerous than usual.

Doing her best to keep her worry confined to the back of her mind, Elizabeth pulled up outside the little cottage with its neat lawn and rose-lined pathway. Thinking of the house she'd visited the day before, she couldn't help comparing Wally's immaculate garden to the rag and bone man's bedraggled efforts.

Reminding herself not to think ill of the dead, she tapped on the front door of the cottage. It opened immediately, revealing Priscilla Carbunkle, her face beaming with pleasure at the sight of her visitor.

"Lady Elizabeth! How good of you to call." She stepped back, saying over her shoulder, "Look, Wally! Look who's come to call!"

Wally's weathered face appeared over her shoulder. "Your ladyship! Come in, come in!"

Warmed by their welcome, Elizabeth stepped into the tidy little parlor, her gaze drawn immediately to the large vase of glorious pink roses that filled the room with their fragrance. "Oh, what beautiful roses! They smell divine."

"You must have some to take home with you, your ladyship." Priscilla led her visitor to a comfortable chair. "Though, of course, I'm sure the Manor House roses are just as lovely."

"Actually they're not," Elizabeth admitted as she seated herself. "Desmond is rather lackadaisical, I'm afraid. How I miss the gardeners we used to have when my parents were alive."

"Indeed," Wally murmured. "Such a great loss for you. I often wonder how you manage in that monumental house without all the servants."

Priscilla gave him a sharp look, which he either didn't see or chose not to acknowledge.

Elizabeth smiled. "Such a very small area of the manor is actually in use these days. We manage very well with Martin and Violet. Then, of course, there's Sadie and Polly, who are a great help."

"Always think of Martin as a doddery old fool," Wally said bluntly. "I'm surprised he's still around."

Obviously embarrassed by her husband's remarks, Priscilla said hastily, "I'll put the kettle on, your ladyship. I'm sure you could do with a nice cup of tea." She vanished into the kitchen, where she could be heard rattling cups and saucers loud enough to indicate her agitation.

Apparently oblivious of his wife's disapproval, Wally beamed at Elizabeth. "Invasion seems to be going well, don't you think? How are your American chaps doing over there? Must be a bit dicey for them in those planes."

"I imagine it is." Elizabeth opened her capacious handbag and drew out a flat square package wrapped in blue crepe paper. "I brought you and Priscilla a small gift for the house. Just to welcome you as a married couple."

She handed it to Wally, who seemed taken aback. "Jolly decent of you, your ladyship, I'm sure. Much obliged. I'll let the little lady open it."

Relieved, Elizabeth watched him lay the package on a table next to his elbow. She'd planned to give the gift to both of them, but she'd needed a distraction in order to avoid discussing the welfare of certain American pilots.

"She needs something to cheer her up," Wally murmured. "Got upset about that mess up at the factory. Nasty business, that."

Surprised, Elizabeth exclaimed, "Oh, did she know Mr. Morgan?"

"Knows the wife. Iris." Wally nodded. "They were good friends at one time, until Clyde started complaining about Iris spending too much time with Prissy. That put the mockers on the friendship, I can tell you." Wally shook his head. "Never did have much time for the bloke. Bit of a nasty temper, he had. Played darts with him a few times and he didn't like losing, that he didn't."

"Not many people do," Elizabeth murmured.

"Ah, but this chap was dashed bombastic about it. Saw him one night swipe a tankard of beer clear off the counter." Wally frowned. "Funny thing, I always thought he was left-handed. Always threw a dart with his left hand, he did. Used to put me off, sometimes, watching him. And then when I saw him lying there with that hole in his head, poor blighter, the gun was in his right hand." Wally shrugged. "I s'pose it makes no difference which hand you use. You're just as dead, right?"

Fortunately Priscilla reappeared at that moment, saving Elizabeth from answering.

Delighted with the gift of tea towels, purchased with much-cherished coupons, Priscilla gushed over them at great length, while Wally nodded and smiled. "We were just talking about Clyde doing himself in," he said when Priscilla had poured the tea. "I was telling her ladyship as how you were friends with Iris until Clyde put a stop to it."

Priscilla's mouth tightened. "Well, yes, that was unfortunate. I feel sorry for Iris. I must go down there and visit with her."

"Well, I for one won't miss him that much." Wally leaned back in his chair, one hand holding his cup and the other a slice of Priscilla's nut cake. "Always bragging, he was. Got tired of that story about how he got shot in the eye, then with only one good eye took a Luger off the German who shot him and killed him with it. Kept saying he was going to bring in the gun to show everyone. I thought he was lying about the whole thing." He shook his head. "Seems ironic, doesn't it? Ends up killing himself with the blasted thing."

"Ironic, indeed," Elizabeth murmured.

Priscilla launched into an account of their honeymoon in the Scottish Highlands, obviously determined to change the subject.

Elizabeth payed scant attention to her. She was still too busy wondering why a man played a serious game of darts with his left hand, then chose to end his life with his right. Something didn't quite fit, and it looked very much as if she had yet another mystery on her hands.

CHAPTER
🎀 6 🎀

"You're not really going after this crackpot, are you?" Polly demanded. Sprawled on Sadie's bed, she watched the housemaid draw her light brown hair into a clump on each side of her head and fasten them with rubber bands. The result always reminded Polly of rabbit ears, but she kept that to herself. Sadie appeared to be thick-skinned, but Polly never knew if she was covering up what she really felt inside.

Sadie had been bombed out of her house during an air raid in London, but despite Polly's encouragement, she never wanted to talk about it. Instead she'd make a funny remark, as if the whole thing were a joke. Polly knew it wasn't, of course. She guessed it was just Sadie's way of coping with what must have been a terrible experience. Which made her wonder what else Sadie kept inside her.

"If we don't find him, no one else will bother," Sadie declared, giving one of the bunches of hair a flick with her fingers. She turned back from the mirror to join Polly on the bed. "You really don't think those nitwits down at the police station will find him, do you? They couldn't find a raisin in a currant bun."

Polly felt a quiver of fear. "So what are you going to do?"

Sadie grinned. "Not me. Us. You and me. We're going to find out who's stealing ladies' drawers from the washing lines. If we don't, we'll never be able to hang our washing out again until he's caught. Not that we've got much underwear left to hang out, anyway."

The fear turned to dread. "How the blazes are we supposed to do that?"

Sadie pulled her feet up onto the bed and hugged her knees. "I got it all worked out. Your mum sleeps all morning, right?"

"Right. She works until five in the morning then comes home and sleeps until the afternoon."

"Well, the knickers disappear off the line in the mornings. So what we do, we hang out a bunch of them at your house, then keep watch to see if someone steals them."

Polly stared at her. "I haven't got a bunch of them. Most of them went off the line."

"Blast." Sadie frowned. "Well, the only thing to do is collect as many pairs as we can from the manor."

"Violet won't let us do that. She already said we weren't to go after the thief."

Sadie dropped her chin to her knees. "Then we'll just have to steal them from other people's lines."

Polly squealed in horror. "We can't do that. They'll put us in prison."

"We'll give them all back later." Sadie lifted her head, her eyes gleaming with excitement. "After all, if the thief gets them first, they wouldn't get them back. We'd be doing everyone a favor. And if we take all the knickers off the lines and put them on yours, then the thief will have to steal them from your line and we'll catch him in the act." She patted her own shoulder. "Brilliant, Sadie. Bloody brilliant."

"Violet doesn't like us saying that word," Polly murmured.

"Piss on Violet." Having thoroughly shocked Polly, she laughed. "Come on, Pol, don't you want to see this bugger put in a loony bin where he belongs?"

"I s'pose so." She really didn't want anything to do with him, but she couldn't tell Sadie that. Sadie was so daring and Polly dearly wanted to be like her, even if it did get them in trouble sometimes. "Maybe if we ask people they'll give us their knickers to put on the line," she suggested hopefully.

"Nah." Sadie's bunches of hair bounced as she shook her head. "They'd be too embarrassed. We'll just have to borrow them and give them back later. They can't call it stealing then. Besides, once we catch the real thief, everyone will be so grateful they'll forgive us anything."

Though she was still nervous about the whole thing, Polly nodded her head. "All right, then. Let's do it." After all, she told herself, she couldn't afford to lose any more underwear. "What will we do if we see him? What if he's big and strong?" Remembering the terrible news about the rag and bone man, she added fearfully, "What if he has a gun and shoots us?"

Sadie clicked her tongue. "Silly, we won't try to grab him or anything. We'll follow him and see where he goes and then we'll tell George where he is."

"Oh." That helped her feel a little better. "All right, then. When?"

"Tomorrow. That's when you'll be collecting the rents, right?"

Polly nodded.

"All right, then. Lady Elizabeth will think you're in the village collecting rents, and Violet never bothers about where I am in the mornings so long as everything's kept clean, so no one will miss us. We'll go down first thing on our bicycles, get as many pairs of drawers as we can find, and bring them back to your house and hang them on the line. Then we'll wait."

It sounded so simple, Polly assured herself. What could possibly go wrong with that?

That afternoon Elizabeth decided to pay Iris Morgan another visit. The roses were in full bloom, and she cut an armful to take with her. After laying them carefully in the sidecar, she soared off into the wind, and arrived a few minutes later at the rag and bone man's house.

Iris took a long time to answer her knock on the front door. So long, in fact, that had it not been for the shrieks Elizabeth could hear coming from behind the house, she would have thought no one was home.

Iris's expression was not at all welcoming, and Elizabeth offered her the bouquet of roses, hoping their heavenly fragrance would soften the other woman's hard features.

Iris thanked her politely, but seemed not at all inclined to invite her visitor inside. Instead, she stood stolidly in the doorway, with an air of someone waiting to be rid of a nuisance.

Determined to accomplish her mission, Elizabeth

summoned a bright smile. "May I come inside for a moment?" she murmured, stepping purposefully toward the door. "There's something I'd like to discuss with you."

The woman's face changed abruptly, and Elizabeth was disturbed by the fear in her eyes. "It's not about the kiddies, is it?" she asked sharply. "You've not come to take them away?"

"Of course not!" Dismayed at causing the woman anxiety, Elizabeth hurried to reassure her. "I simply wanted to talk to you about your late husband."

Just then a clatter of footsteps warned Elizabeth that someone else was coming up the pathway behind her, apparently in a great hurry. Turning to confront the newcomer, she saw a young boy, wearing frayed trousers and a faded shirt. He stopped short at the sight of her, his gaze shifting to the woman behind her.

"This is my son," Iris said quietly. To the boy she added, "Come and pay your respects to Lady Elizabeth, Tommy."

Elizabeth smiled at the boy, who answered her with a sullen look and mumbled something she couldn't catch.

"Sorry, your ladyship," Iris said quickly. "He's upset about his father."

Tommy started to turn away and she added, "Where are you going? I need you to look after your sister. She's out there in the back garden by herself."

The boy hesitated, then shrugged and started down the path that led around the house. He had to pass quite close to Elizabeth, and she felt a pang of dismay when she saw dark purple bruises along his jaw. She waited until he was out of earshot before saying to Iris, "Those bruises look quite painful."

Iris met her gaze for a minute or so before answering. "Always fighting, he is. Got in a scrap with his mates this morning."

Elizabeth watched the boy disappear. "I wonder what makes children feel they have to settle things with their fists."

Iris looked uncomfortable. "Boys will be boys, I suppose." She opened the door a little wider. "You'd better come inside, your ladyship. I have soup on the stove, and I don't want it boiling over."

Elizabeth stepped over the threshold, and caught sight of the cat's tail as it disappeared under the chair. Iris excused herself and disappeared into the kitchen.

Seizing the moment, Elizabeth moved over to where the photograph of Clyde Morgan sat on the sideboard. Peering at it, she noted the raised left hand holding the dart. Wally had been right about that, at least.

"He wasn't a handsome man by any means," Iris said quietly behind her. "But he was my husband and the father of my children and he did his best."

Spinning around, Elizabeth said quickly, "Oh, I'm quite sure he did." Iris's eyes were bleak with misery and she felt an ache of sympathy. "You must miss him dreadfully." She gestured at the photograph. "Was he left-handed with everything, or just when he was playing darts?"

Iris shot her a strange look. "He was left-handed with everything. Why do you ask?"

Elizabeth hesitated, then sat down on the edge of the settee. "Mrs. Morgan, when your husband was found, he was holding the gun in his right hand. Does that seem strange to you?"

Iris's face turned quite white. "So what are you saying?"

"I'm not sure." Elizabeth paused, then added, "I'd like to hear exactly what happened when your husband accidentally hit that young girl in the head with a dart."

Iris sank on the chair opposite her. "There's not much to tell. Clyde was playing a darts match at the Tudor Arms, and someone spoke to him just as he was about to throw. His hand jerked, the dart slipped in his fingers and went off in the wrong direction. It hit Sheila Redding in the head. The judge said it were an accident."

Up until then her voice had been low and flat, as if reciting a well-rehearsed piece of information. But now her voice rose, and sharpened. "It *were* an accident, your ladyship. I'd swear to that. My Clyde would never have deliberately thrown a dart at anyone. He had a bit of a temper and he was a bit hard on the kiddies sometimes, but he wasn't vicious. He really wasn't."

Elizabeth had to admire the way the woman defended her husband. "I understand Miss Redding is in a home in North Horsham?"

Iris nodded. "I used to go and see her sometimes, but she got so upset I stopped going. Her mum and dad still live here in Sitting Marsh. As a matter of fact, I saw Bob Redding the other day. I suppose he must be home on leave. I feel so sad for them both. To have a child like that and see her so helpless. It must be heartbreaking for them."

"I'm sure it is." Elizabeth stood. "Thank you, Mrs. Morgan. I appreciate you talking to me."

Iris walked with her to the door. "About this gun being in Clyde's right hand . . ." She hesitated, then rushed on, "You're not thinking someone else might have shot him, like Mr. Redding, for instance? I really don't think he'd do that, m'm. Really I don't. I don't know the Reddings very well, but they seem like very nice people. I don't know why Clyde used his right hand to shoot himself, but he did a lot of things I never understood."

Elizabeth studied her anxious face. "You may be right, Mrs. Morgan. Then again, who knows what any of us are capable of when fighting our demons?"

Iris's eyes filled with tears again. "I just wish there was something I could have done to prevent all this."

"We can't always be there for the ones we love," Elizabeth said softly. "No matter how much we want to be. We can't be responsible for their actions, nor blame ourselves when something goes wrong. We can only pray for them."

Iris gave her a wobbly smile through her tears. "Oh, I do that, your ladyship. Every day of my life."

"And so do I." Turning her back on the tearful woman, Elizabeth walked purposefully down the garden path.

The weekly meeting of the Housewives League was a little late getting started that afternoon. Crowded into Rita Crumm's dinky front room, the women were avidly discussing the death of the rag and bone man, each of them embellishing on the details they'd heard.

"Shot himself with his own gun," Marge Gunther declared, her chubby arm jerking up to imitate someone raising a gun to his head. "Blew his bloomin' brains out all over the floor, he did." Marge's voice was powerful, overriding the rest of the chatter.

Florrie Evans, a fluttery little woman, squealed at

this statement and slapped her hands over her mouth, eyes wide above her fingers.

"Must have been that German gun he was always talking about," Clara Rigglesby announced. She was Marge's best friend and secretly thought Marge should be the leader of the Housewives League instead of bossy Rita Crumm.

Rita chose that moment to make her entrance. She always waited until everyone was assembled before striding into the room to restore order. Rita loved to bring everyone to order. She was very proud of the league and the work they did for the war effort, and considered herself something of a hero for leading her stalwart, though often reluctant, members into battle.

If anyone could be credited for winning the war on the home front, Rita was determined to be in the front line. She ruled with an iron fist, and heaven help anyone who opposed her. Her greatest regret was that she wasn't born a lady of the manor. She was convinced she would have done a far better job than Lady Elizabeth Hartleigh Compton.

Upon perceiving that no one had taken any notice of her carefully timed entrance, Rita remedied the situation by screeching at the top of her lungs, "Ladies! Order, please!"

She was gratified when the chattering women fell silent. She would have been a lot happier had they done that the second she stepped through the door, but she'd been leading this mob long enough not to expect miracles.

She was about to make her first announcement—a reminder that the annual summer fete was drawing near and she was expecting a larger amount of handmade goods this year—when, out of the blue, Marge piped up.

"We was talking about the rag and bone man blowing his brains out."

Rita tightened her thin lips, which had the effect of making them disappear entirely. She found Marge irritating, especially when she was trying to agitate with her outrageous statements.

"Instead of gossiping about the wretched man like a bunch of starving vultures," Rita said primly, "you should be feeling sorry for the poor widow. It could happen to any of us, you know. Losing a husband, I mean."

The reminder that their absent husbands might not come home from the war was enough to subdue the women for a moment. But only for a moment.

Rita had barely begun to launch into her carefully prepared speech when Marge said clearly, "Well, I'm not so sure he did kill himself."

Even Rita was stunned by this remark. She turned her piercing glare on Marge. "What on earth does that mean?"

Marge, who had arrived last as usual and had to resort to sitting on the floor, stretched out her legs in front of her. "I ran into Priscilla Pierce this morning and—"

"She's not Prissy Pierce anymore," Nellie Smith said, with a trace of bitterness. Nellie, the only unmarried member of the league, made no secret of the fact she envied Priscilla, even if she had married a gent old enough to be Nellie's father.

"Priscilla Carbunkle, then," Marge said, starting to giggle. "That's a mouthful and a half, ain't it?"

"Never mind that," Rita said, her voice sharp with impatience. "What did you mean about Clyde Morgan not shooting himself?"

Basking in the glory of attention, Marge gave her a smug smile. "Well, Priscilla said as how Wally saw the body lying in the ruins." She rolled her eyes. "All bloody he were, with half his head blown away."

Florrie squealed again, louder this time, and a chatter arose among the women, almost drowning out Rita's harsh command.

"Quiet! Quiet, I say!" She waited for order to be restored, then, as the women in the room fell silent, she addressed Marge again. "If you can't explain what you mean without all these gory details, then we don't want to know."

"Oh, all right." Marge wiggled her feet in her sensible walking shoes. "Well, Priscilla said that Wally saw the gun in his hand and it was in his right hand. Everyone knows that Clyde Morgan was left-handed."

"I didn't know that," Nellie muttered.

"Well, I did." Marge glared at her.

"You said everyone knows."

"I thought everyone did know."

"Shut *up!*" Rita roared. "Get on with it, Marge, or else be quiet and let the rest of us get on with the important matters."

Marge shrugged. "Well, all I'm saying is, if the rag and bone man was left-handed, why would he use his right hand to shoot himself? You'd think it would be more natural to use the hand he always uses, wouldn't you?"

Nellie stared at her. "Are you saying someone *else* shot him?"

Marge took her time answering, looking from one stunned face to another. "Well, what do *you* think?"

"Oh, my," Florrie whispered. "He was *murdered*?"

"By a German gun," Clara said solemnly.

Rita caught her breath. "A German gun? That means we could have another German spy among us."

"Or maybe a German pilot, like the one what bailed out over the village green that time," Nellie suggested.

Grasping at the frail straw in her own inimitable way, Rita prepared to turn it into a haystack. "Well, I think this calls for action from the Housewives League. If there's another German skulking around the village, it's up to us to ferret him out and hand him over to the authorities."

Marge groaned. "Not again."

Rita lifted her chin. "What was that, Marjorie? You have an objection to us doing our duty?"

All heads turned toward Marge, hoping to see a battle ensue.

Disappointing them, Marge merely shrugged. "Nothing. It's just that I remember the last time we went looking for Germans. Almost got an innocent bird-watcher killed, we did."

"What about the time before," Nellie reminded Rita, "when the German pilot hid in the windmill? Almost got your daughter killed that time."

"Nah," Clara said happily. "She was sneaking him food and drink, remember?"

All eyes switched to Rita, whose cheeks burned with resentment. *Stupid woman,* she thought, *what did she have to bring that up for?* "Never mind all that," she said hurriedly. "Both times there really was a German in Sitting Marsh, wasn't there?"

A chorus of reluctant agreement answered her.

"Very well, then. We start looking for this one. After all, if it wasn't for us, no one would even know there was one lurking about."

After thinking about it for a moment or two, Rita couldn't exactly remember how they came to know there was one this time, but she didn't let that stop her. After all the excitement of the factory blowing up had died down, things had been pretty quiet in Sitting Marsh. She was just dying to get her hands on something else to get excited about, and a possible German spy in their presence, no matter how vague the details, was the perfect answer to her prayers.

CHAPTER
❀ 7 ❀

"It's like I always said, give a man enough rope, he'll end up hanging hisself." George nodded to emphasize his words.

Elizabeth, seated opposite him on the miserably uncomfortable chair, frowned. "I really don't think that applies to Clyde Morgan, George. As I've said, the fact that the gun was found in his right hand raises some questions, don't you think?"

George passed a hand over his head, a habit which Elizabeth suspected had contributed greatly to the fact that he was almost completely bald. "He'd probably been boozing. Men do some very strange things when they're sozzled."

"That's as may be." Elizabeth shifted her hips to a more comfortable position. "But I maintain that if he was in a befuddled state, as you suggest, his actions would be automatic, would they not? His actual decision might well have been reached under the influence of alcohol, but if I picture a man hopeless enough to end his own life, surely he would make that last desperate move in a way most natural to him. He would reach for the gun with his left hand. I'm convinced of it."

"Well, we'll never know now, will we." George leaned back in his chair and laced his stubby fingers together across his chest. "Iris Morgan has identified the gun as the one belonging to her husband, and the inspector is satisfied it were suicide, so the case is closed."

Elizabeth pinched her lips together. "Don't you find it odd that the man should choose such a dismal place for his last act on earth? All alone, in the ruins of a deserted building?"

Obviously put out by her insistence, George gave her a baleful look. "I find it odd, your ladyship, that anyone would take a gun and blow his brains out. That's what's odd. Poor sod must have been in a terrible state to do such a thing. As for where he did it, well, I'd say he chose that place because he thought no one would find him and know what he'd done. He knew the building was coming down. Sort of a burial place for him, weren't it."

"And you think that Clyde Morgan, from all accounts a harsh bully of a man with a temper to be feared, worried about what people would think of him if they knew he'd killed himself?"

George dropped his hands to the table. "I didn't think you knew the gentleman, your ladyship."

"I didn't," Elizabeth said shortly. "But from everything I've heard and seen, it wasn't that difficult to draw that conclusion."

"If you're talking about that dart incident—"

"I'm talking about a little girl who bullies her toys in an obvious imitation of her father. And a young boy who finds it necessary to settle his differences by pummeling his friends. I'm talking about at least two people who have mentioned Clyde Morgan's hot temper. What other conclusion would you have me reach?"

George's eyes grew wary. "What are you saying, exactly?"

"I'm saying that from what I've heard, Clyde Morgan was a man who collected enemies. I'm saying there's a strong possibility that someone else shot him and made it look like suicide. The distraught father of a helpless young woman, for instance."

George's eyes widened. "Bob Redding?" He shook his head violently. "No, no, your ladyship. You're on the wrong track there. I won't argue that he was upset by the unfortunate accident, but he's not the kind of man who'd take a gun to someone's head. Besides, this all happened almost two years ago. If Bob was going to do something like that he would have done it before this."

"Not necessarily," Elizabeth said grimly. "Two years of watching your daughter struggle to hang on to life can create a monster out of the most docile of men."

"Well, no matter what you or I think, the inspector is satisfied it's suicide." George leaned forward to emphasize his point. "I suggest, for everyone's peace of mind, your ladyship, that you leave it at that."

Elizabeth rose. "I shall keep your suggestion in mind, George. Thank you for your time." She swept out, while George was still struggling to his feet.

She had no attention of heeding his unwanted advice, of course. Until she was fully satisfied that every avenue had been explored, she was not about to accept the verdict of a police inspector who rarely had time to visit Sitting Marsh, much less actually work on a case.

The demands of a big town like North Horsham kept the inspector's hands too full for him to worry about an insignificant little village where the death of a man could so easily be dismissed as self-inflicted. That infuriated her. If Clyde Morgan was murdered by someone else's hand, then justice had to be done, and it appeared that once more it would be up to her to ferret out the truth.

The saloon bar of the Tudor Arms was empty when Elizabeth entered a few minutes later. It was shortly before opening time, and she knew Alfie would be setting up the bar, though the customers would not arrive until another half hour or so—the official time when Alfie could start serving the beer.

From then on, the ancient rafters of the centuries-old building would echo with the shouts, cheers, tinkling piano keys, and bawdy songs of the rowdy crowd filling the room.

Elizabeth usually made sure to be gone before that happened. Not that she had anything against drinking, of course. In fact, Alfie always kept a bottle of her favorite sherry under the counter for her, ready to pour a quick one whenever she wandered in. Her early departures reflected more her reluctance to be seen hobnobbing in such doubtful company.

Once the American GIs found the pub, they'd made it a favorite spot to relax, drink, play darts, and flirt with the village girls. It wasn't long before word had spread to North Horsham, and a fair proportion of the female population of that town rode the bus all the way to Sitting Marsh to indulge in what had become a national pastime for a large number of British ladies—meeting Yanks.

This was looked upon by older, more staid, and for the most part envious residents as unacceptable behavior. Everyone knew the Yanks were "overpaid, oversexed, and over here," and if a young lady, or in some cases one more mature in years and married to boot, was reckless enough to keep company with a Yank, her reputation immediately became tarnished, and furtive whispers followed her wherever she went. This was not an environment in which the lady of the manor should indulge, as Violet was constantly reminding her.

Nevertheless, Alfie, who was the recipient of more than one juicy secret disclosed while under the influence of several pints of ale, was an unsurpassed source of information that was, more often than not, concealed from the long arm of the law. Therefore Elizabeth felt justified in her illicit jaunts to the pub.

Alfie greeted her with his usual enthusiasm and brought out the half-full bottle of sherry. "Been saving this for you, your ladyship," he announced with a cheerful grin. "Don't know when I'll get any more, so I've been telling the ladies I'm out of it."

"That's very good of you, Alfie." Elizabeth settled herself at the empty bar. "I appreciate the gesture, and I hope it won't get you into any trouble."

Alfie laughed. "I don't think anyone's going to object to me saving a spot of sherry for the lady of the manor."

"I don't like to think I'm privileged. Wartime is a great equalizer, and I must sacrifice just as much as everyone else."

"I reckon you do your share of sacrificing, m'm." Alfie poured a generous shot of golden liquid into the slender glass. "You do a lot for the people of this village, always calling on them and taking little extras for the ones who need it. Not to mention putting your neck out now and then when the constables are too thick to see what needs to be done."

"Ah, speaking of which . . ." Elizabeth lifted her glass and took a sip of sherry. The deliciously smooth liquid warmed her throat, and she let it slide down before finishing the sentence. "I was wondering if you happened to see Clyde Morgan in here the night before last?"

"Aha!" Alfie nodded his head, picked up a glass tankard, and began polishing it. "I wondered when you'd get around to that. Soon as I heard about Clyde being found dead yesterday, I knew sooner or later you'd be around asking questions."

Elizabeth studied his face. "So you don't think Clyde shot himself?"

"I didn't say that." Alfie kept his gaze on the tankard, which seemed to glow under the frenzied friction of his polishing cloth. "All I'm saying is that Clyde Morgan was not in some people's good books. I wouldn't be at all surprised if someone didn't bump him off."

Elizabeth took another sip of sherry. The drink had reached her stomach now and was spreading warmth throughout her body. A most pleasant feeling indeed. "Anyone in particular?"

Alfie shot her a glance under bushy brows. "A lot of people were fed up with him. He liked his beer, and when he was drinking, he got loud and nasty. Folks didn't like that. He was a liar, too. Always shooting his mouth off about being shot in the eye by a German soldier. Truth is, he lost that eye in a pub brawl in France early in the war. Got hit with a flying bottle. He must have forgot he told me about that one."

Elizabeth shuddered. "How awful. No wonder he was bad-tempered."

"He was the one what started it, by all accounts." Alfie put down the tankard and picked up another one. "I was getting a bit worried about him a couple of nights ago when he was in here. Swallowing beer like it was his last day on earth, he was." He paused in his polishing. "Blimey, come to think of it, it *were* his last day on earth."

"Did he have an argument with anyone that night?"

"Not that I can recall. Bit quiet it were. I think I'd have known if there'd been any nasty business in here." He began buffing the tankard again. "Like that night a few weeks back. A young kid traded his dead father's army pistol to Clyde for a hunting knife. Two days later the kid cut himself in the arm. He got an artery, and bled to death before his mother could get help for him. She came down here after Clyde one night, crying and carrying on. Said it were all Clyde's fault and she'd see he paid for it."

"Oh, dear. I do remember reading about that poor child in the paper," Elizabeth said. "Rose Clovell's son, Arnie. I went down to visit his mother. Poor woman, she was beside herself with grief. She'd only recently lost her husband, then to lose a son like that . . . What a tragedy."

"That's her. Then there's Bob Redding. His daughter's in a wheelchair because of Clyde. 'Course, it was an accident, but if he hadn't been drinking, he'd never have chucked a dart the wrong way and hit her in the head."

"Dreadful," Elizabeth agreed. "George did mention

that incident to me. I understand Mr. Redding is home on leave right now?"

"That's right." Alfie lifted the glass and inspected it. "Got wounded in the invasion. He's back home recovering."

"Perhaps I'll pay him a visit," Elizabeth murmured. "Just to see how well he's doing."

"Might not be a bad idea, your ladyship." Alfie nodded at her glass. "Another one?"

"I don't think so, thank you." She slid off the stool. "I must be getting home for supper, or Violet will no doubt give me a lecture."

Alfie nodded. "How's that major of yours? Back from the invasion yet?"

Elizabeth did her best to hide her distress. "Not yet, Alfie. I expect they are all being kept busy at the base."

"I only asked because I saw some of his boys go by here in their jeeps a little while ago. I wondered if he was with them. They'll probably be in later. Must say I've missed them. It's been really quiet without them all singing and carrying on in here. The girls have missed them, too. Keep asking me when they're coming back, they do."

Elizabeth fought for breath, before saying faintly, "Oh, I didn't know they were back. I'll have to alert Violet to air the beds for them."

Alfie grinned. "Reckon they'll warm them up themselves once they get a few pints of beer inside them."

"Excuse me," Elizabeth said abruptly. "I must run." She was out of the door before Alfie had finished saying good-bye.

• • •

The long summer evenings were cherished by everyone. Unhampered by the restrictions of the blackout, people enjoyed a freedom they were denied during the endless, miserable dark days of winter.

Normally Elizabeth would linger on her way home to enjoy the gold and orange hues of the setting sun, or watch the evening mists gather over the downs and settle in the branches of the oak trees. Often she would pause on the edge of the cliffs and gaze over the barbed wire at the vast ocean and the black velvet of the night sky crawling toward the shore.

This evening, however, she had but one thought in mind—to return home with as much haste as possible. Earl's officers were back in town, and that meant he could have returned as well.

Regretting the time she'd wasted, Elizabeth roared up the curving driveway and into the courtyard. Her leap of hope when she saw several jeeps parked near the stables made her quite breathless.

Heart pounding, she scrambled off her motorcycle, paying scant heed to the rise of her skirt, which surely would have raised Violet's eyebrows clear into her scalp. In a fever of impatience, she wheeled the machine into the stable and parked it there.

The birds were so loud outside in the courtyard she could hear them from where she stood in the shadows of the empty stalls. The tiny creatures filled the air with a heavenly chorus of warbling and twittering that echoed across the quiet peace of the countryside.

Smiling at the sound, Elizabeth was about to step out into the fading sunlight when a pair of hands settled on her shoulders. Her startled shriek resounded in the rafters of the ancient building, sending a mouse scurrying for cover.

She whirled around, her breath catching in her throat, for there he was, his eyes crinkling at the corners as he smiled down at her.

Until that moment, she hadn't realized the depth of her fear for his safety. She uttered a cry and without another thought, went into his arms. He cradled her, one hand stroking her hair while she unashamedly bawled against his shoulder.

He said nothing until her tears were spent, then as she pulled away from him, he said gently, "Feel better? I didn't mean to scare you. I heard your motorbike coming up the driveway and I just wanted to surprise you."

"I know." She hiccuped and turned it into a little laugh. "I have no earthly idea why I'm crying. It's just that . . ." Her voice broke and she paused, waiting for her composure to reassert itself.

"It's okay if you cry," Earl said, folding his hands around hers. "I've seen plenty of grown men cry, believe me."

"I'm sure you have." Her voice still trembled, but she struggled on. "It's just that I worried so much about you, and there was no word from you and I thought . . . I was afraid . . ."

"I'm sorry. Everything was shut down tight at the base. No one could call out."

She searched his face, trying to see behind the smile to what really lay beneath. "It must have been so awful for you—"

He stopped her with a quick shake of his head.

"Let's not talk about it now. I'm back, for a little while, anyway. Let's just enjoy the time while we can."

"How long?"

Her spirits sank when he said, with a trace of apology, "I have to be back first thing in the morning."

Her anger took her by surprise. So little time. The war had a big enough claim on him, surely they could spare him a little while longer. Where was the empathy, the understanding that a man must surely break if pushed to the limits?

One had only to look deep into his eyes to see the anguish and the agony of all that he had been through, all that he had seen. Earl Monroe had great compassion for his fellow man. He would not take lightly the loss of so many.

"You know what I want?" He lifted her hands to his mouth and pressed his lips to her fingers. "I want to sit in that comfortable old rocker of yours with a double scotch and listen to everything you've been up to since I've been away."

She chased away her disappointment with a smile. "And so you shall. You must join me for supper tonight. I'm sure Violet will be able to rustle up something halfway edible."

He grinned. "Missed the steaks, huh?"

"With a passion." She linked her arm through his, then paused, almost afraid to ask the question. "What about Joe Hanson? Is he . . . ?" She let her voice trail off, unable to finish.

Earl squeezed her hand. "The last time I saw him, which was about an hour ago, he had your housemaid wrapped around his neck."

Her breath came out in a rush of relief. "Oh, thank

heavens. Sadie would be absolutely devastated if something happened to him."

"I guess she would." His voice was teasing when he added, "How about you? How devastated would you be?"

She deliberately misinterpreted his question. "Well, of course I would be terribly devastated. Joe Hanson is a very nice young man and I—"

He stopped short at the bottom of the steps and turned her around to face him. "You know very well what I meant."

He was so close she could feel the warmth from his body. She had never wanted anything in her life as much as she wanted his mouth on hers. She tried to brush off the moment with a light laugh. "And you know very well how devastated I would be. I just don't like to talk about it, that's all."

"Then let's not waste time talking."

He took her by surprise, pulling her against him while his mouth sought hers. For one fleeting second she worried that someone might see them, then the world and its worries faded from her mind as she gave herself up to the pure pleasure of his embrace.

CHAPTER

❈ 8 ❈

Minutes later Elizabeth sat with Earl in the conservatory, trying to calm her jittery nerves while Violet fussed and dithered over him. Considering her undisguised disapproval of their relationship, Elizabeth thought with some amusement that her housekeeper was going to great pains to welcome him home.

"I have just the thing for supper," Violet announced. "I was saving this dish for a special occasion, and for the life of me I can't think of a better reason to celebrate than right now."

She beamed at Earl as she handed him his scotch. "We're all so terribly proud of what everyone did over there in the invasion, Major, that we are. From what we've heard on the wireless, we're beating back the Germans, and we won't stop until we're all the way to Berlin. They're saying we've turned the corner at last."

Earl smiled, but his eyes were bleak. "Let's hope

they're right, Violet. This darn war has gone on long enough."

Something about the way he said it struck a chill in Elizabeth's heart. She knew there was no point in questioning him. He would tell her what he could. The feeling that he was keeping something significant from her, however, disturbed her more than she wanted to admit.

Violet disappeared out the door, leaving them alone in a strained silence. Finally Earl spoke. "Penny for them?"

She shook her head. "Oh, it's nothing. I was just thinking of all you must have gone through these last few days."

"It was nothing compared to the boys on the beaches. They're the real heroes. All we could do was try to blast the hell out of the enemy. It wasn't enough, but it was the best we could do."

Very modest, considering the reports she'd heard about the planes flying dangerously low into enemy fire to carry out their mission. "And now what?"

He looked down at his glass, swirling the liquor around like a miniature whirlpool. "Paris. We have to liberate Paris. I'm afraid it's going to be a long, bloody battle before we get there."

The fear that was always with her intensified. "I suppose you'll be flying missions into France and Germany."

"I thought we weren't going to talk about the war."

She pushed the fear away as best she could. "You're right, of course. You need this time to clear your mind and think about other things."

"So tell me what you've been up to since I've been gone. No chasing after murderers, I hope?"

Elizabeth picked up her glass of sherry. "Well, now that you mention it . . ."

Earl's face changed and he quickly put down his glass. "Don't tell me—"

"I'm not exactly sure at this point." Elizabeth took a sip of her sherry. "It could be murder, or it could be suicide." She told him how Clyde Morgan's body was found in the ruins of the factory, and that the gun was in his right hand. "There are at least two people who might have had a reason to want him dead," she finished, "and by all accounts, there could be more. He wasn't a very likeable man."

"That doesn't mean they killed him."

"No, but it seems strange to me that he would use his weakest hand to kill himself, and choose a place to do it where his body might not have been discovered for some time, if at all. People usually kill themselves to make a statement. They want to be found. Most of all, though, Clyde Morgan doesn't strike me as the sort of person who would kill himself. Bullies don't usually have that much courage."

Earl nodded gravely, his gaze concentrated on her face. "I guess this means you're gonna go digging and getting into trouble again."

"I don't go looking for trouble," Elizabeth said with a touch of resentment. "I go looking for the truth. Unfortunately in most cases someone else is determined to keep the truth from me. That's where the trouble begins."

"Exactly." Earl reached for her hand. "I reckon I'd be wasting my breath to suggest you leave this one to the cops."

"Absolutely." She saw the concern in his eyes and

smiled fondly at him. "Don't worry about me, Earl. I promise I'll be careful."

"Where have I heard that before?" He lifted her hand and brushed her fingers with his lips. "I won't be around for the next few days to keep an eye on you. That worries me."

"You have enough to worry about." She curled her fingers around his, then hastily pulled them away from him when a tap on the door announced Violet's entrance.

"I'll be serving your meal in the dining room in five minutes," she said, with an approving nod at Earl.

Elizabeth stared at her in surprise. "You're serving dinner? Where's Martin, then?"

Violet avoided her gaze. "In his room, I suppose. He looked tired, so I thought I'd let him rest. I don't mind serving dinner for once."

"Great!" Earl said, rising to his feet. "I'm starving." He held out a hand to assist Elizabeth. "What's for supper?"

"Corned beef rissoles."

The door closed behind her, and Elizabeth almost laughed out loud at the expression on Earl's face.

"What the heck is that?"

"I have no idea. One of Violet's new recipes. She got a book of them from the Ministry of Food, and she's been trying them out on us. Some of them are quite disgusting, but considering how scarce good food has become, we have to make do with what we've got."

"In that case, I'll pretend it's steak." He took her hand and linked her arm through his. "As long as I have a lovely lady to keep me company, I don't care what I eat."

She made a face at him. "That's what I love about

you Americans. You truly know how to make a lady feel thoroughly appreciated."

He dropped his voice to a low drawl that sounded suspiciously like a bad imitation of Humphrey Bogart. "I could make you feel a lot more appreciated, sweetheart, if you weren't so damn worried about protocol."

She hid her agitation behind feigned indignation. "Why, Major! Whatever are you suggesting?"

He grinned, and his voice returned to normal. "As if you didn't know."

Her heart skipped a beat, and she made a big display of hustling him to the door. "Violet will be most annoyed with us if we're not seated when she serves the meal."

"Then let's not keep Violet waiting."

The light tone was still obvious, but she saw regret flicker across his face before he opened the door and allowed her to pass through. The observation depressed her. If only he knew how much she wanted to forget who she was, and why she had to guard her reputation so fiercely.

If only he knew that her heart ached to have more, and that each time she said good-bye she bitterly regretted the time that was being frittered away. She couldn't tell him, of course. For if he knew how close she was to thumbing her nose at protocol, he might very well be tempted to forget his promise to her, and that would be disastrous for all concerned.

Watching Violet serve the meal, Elizabeth felt uneasy about Martin's absence. Violet was hiding something, she could tell. For a fleeting moment she allowed herself to worry about that, but then she put it from her mind. This was her night, hers and Earl's, and she wasn't about to let anything spoil it.

Instead, she spent the precious evening listening to his stories of a wild, wonderful place called Wyoming, laughing at his jokes, and trying not to fall any deeper in love with him than she already was.

True to his word, he ate Violet's latest concoction with as much relish as if he were devouring a steak. Watching him chase the slightly burned, odd-shaped rissoles around his plate, Elizabeth's heart warmed with gratitude for his willingness to make the most of every situation. Just being with him was always such a joy, and if she had to be content with that, then so be it.

When Violet came in to collect the empty plates, Earl handed his up to her with a smile that brought a pink glow to the crotchety housekeeper's cheeks. "That was swell, Violet," he announced, with a heartiness that sounded quite sincere. "There's nothing like a good home-cooked meal to make a man forget his troubles."

"Glad you liked it," Violet muttered. "It was just corned beef, mixed up with mashed potatoes and veggies."

"Very tasty." Earl smacked his lips. "Reminded me of the hamburgers back home, or maybe sausage patties."

"Hamburgers?" Elizabeth stared at him. "What on earth is that?"

Violet paused in the doorway, looking back over her shoulder. "Isn't that what we call mince?"

Now Earl seemed confused. "Mince?"

"Minced-up beef," Violet explained.

Earl's expression lightened. "Yep, that's a hamburger. We shape it in a flat circle, slap it in a bun, and eat it out of our hand. Kind of like the way you guys eat fish and chips. Except we don't eat them out of newspaper."

"Maybe you should try the rissoles that way," Elizabeth suggested.

Violet looked pleased. "Maybe I will."

She disappeared again and Elizabeth smiled at Earl. "That was nice of you, considering they were pretty awful."

"They weren't that bad."

"Wait until you taste Violet's Woolton pie." She told him about the comments that were made at the table when Violet served the pie, and was delighted by his hearty laughter. How she loved to make him laugh. If she could make him forget, even for a moment, the dreadful danger awaiting him, then any sacrifice she had to make was well worth while.

She would walk to the ends of the earth to make him happy. Even if it meant she could expect nothing in return. Just as long as she could be with him, like this. For she strongly suspected this was all she could ever have.

No matter how much she told herself that his pending divorce was the reason she couldn't allow their relationship to go any further, deep down she knew there was a more profound reason. It was her fear that held them at arm's length.

Fear of loving him too much and then losing him, fear of losing everything—her home, her heritage, her self-respect, her place in the community. She had so much to lose, and her fear was a chasm so wide she couldn't see across it, much less bridge it.

All she could do was make the most of every second she was in his company, and hope that the memories would be enough to sustain her during the long, empty years ahead without him.

His good-night kiss was bittersweet, and she hugged the memory of it until she fell asleep.

She awoke the next morning with the usual feeling of dread, and did her best to reassure herself. He had always come back. He would do so again.

She found Violet in her usual spot in the kitchen, at the stove with a cup of tea in one hand while she stirred porridge with the other.

Elizabeth greeted her and sat down at the table, reaching for the newspaper as was her habit. "Have you seen Martin this morning?" she murmured as she scanned the headlines. As usual, they were about the war and the slow, agonizing progress across France.

The photograph of a demolished airplane did nothing to calm her already jumpy nerves, and she raised her head sharply when Violet answered.

"You might as well know, Lizzie. Martin disappeared again last night. He hasn't slept in his bed. I looked in there half an hour ago and he wasn't there."

Elizabeth laid down the newspaper with cold hands. "Where can he be? Where can he possibly go that would keep him out all night?"

"I'd like to know how he gets to where he's going," Violet said, thumping the teakettle down a little too hard on the stove. "He can't walk any faster than a tortoise with lumbago. By the time he gets to the end of the driveway he's on his knees. He can't ride a bicycle or drive a car, even if he had one to drive."

"What about the raffle ticket lady?" Elizabeth frowned. "I can't remember her name."

"You mean Beatrice Carr?" Violet poured tea into a cup, then carried it in its saucer to the table, where she put it down in front of Elizabeth. "I haven't seen her in ages. What about her?"

"Well, she was always asking Martin to go with her somewhere. I just wondered if perhaps he was spending time with her."

Violet's laugh was pure scorn. "Frightened to death of her, he is. He'd never go anywhere with that hussy. Besides, she rides on the bus from North Horsham. Martin wouldn't be able to walk that far to the bus stop in the village." She shook her head. "Blinking mystery it all is, I tell you. Why won't he tell us where he's been? He must know we're worried about him, the silly old goat."

"Well, either he's spending the night at the end of the driveway or someone is meeting him there in a car and taking him somewhere."

Violet's hands jerked, spilling her tea down the sides of her cup. "I never thought of that. Who do you think it is, then? Who does he know that has a car?"

"I have no idea," Elizabeth said quietly. "But one way or another, I intend to find out."

"How many pairs of knickers did you bring?" Polly muttered as Sadie piled the underwear in the kitchen sink. "They can't be all yours."

"They're not." Sadie turned on the tap and filled the sink with cold water. "Some are mine, some are her ladyship's, and some are Violet's. I grabbed every pair I could find."

Polly gasped. "You really went through Lady Elizabeth's drawers?"

"Why not? She'll thank me when we catch the thief. These are all clean, so all we have to do is get them wet, wring them out, and peg them on the line. They'll dry before your mum wakes up, unless the thief takes them, in which case, when we catch him, everyone will thank us."

"Why do we have to get them all wet, anyway? Why can't we just hang them on the line dry?"

"Because the thief might be watching us hang them up and if he grabs them right away and finds them dry he'll know we're setting a trap for him and he'll scarper, won't he."

"Well, Ma won't thank you for waking her up so keep your bloomin' voice down." Polly sent a nervous glance at the door. Her mother was asleep in the bedroom at the top of the stairs. If she woke up and saw what they were doing there'd be hell to pay.

"All right," Sadie muttered. "Here, help me wring these out." She held out a dripping pair of navy blue bloomers.

Polly took them, wrinkling her nose. "These have to be Violet's. They must come down to her knees."

"They do. I've seen them when she bends over."

Polly giggled. "Go on. Whatcha doing staring at Violet's bloomers, then?"

"Can't miss them, can I." Sadie took a pair of pink lace-trimmed drawers and twisted them in a knot.

"Don't you think we should put other washing on the line as well?" Polly squeezed with all her might. The wool bloomers were heavy and hard to wring out. "Won't the thief think it strange that there's only knickers on the line?"

Sadie shrugged. "Those kind of men don't think straight, do they. All he'll see is knickers and he'll grab them."

For the first time Polly felt a stab of fear. "Here, what if he's barmy and he goes after us with a blinking knife or something?"

"That's why we have to make sure he don't see us."
Sadie laid the drawers on the draining board and reached
for another pair. "We'll just follow him until he stops
somewhere and we can see where he lives. Then we can
tell George and Sid to bring him in."

"What if—" Polly broke off as a faint voice called
out from upstairs. "Polly? Is that you?"

Polly shook her head fiercely at Sadie, then opened
the door. "It's all right, Ma, it's only me."

Her mother's voice drifted down the stairs. "What
are you doing home this time of day?"

"I had to collect the rents, Ma. I just stopped in to get
a woolly. It's a bit chilly at the manor this morning."

"All right, then." This was followed by the soft sound
of a door closing.

Polly waited a moment longer, then shut the kitchen
door. "Let's get this lot outside," she whispered, "before
Ma comes down to see what we're doing."

Sadie gathered up the wet washing. "You get the
pegs," she whispered back. "I'll take these."

Polly followed her outside and breathed a sigh of relief as she closed the back door behind her. Grabbing
the peg bag off the clothesline, she muttered, "I hope
we're not wasting our blinking time. What if he won't
come out in daylight? I don't want to sit here all night
waiting for him."

"Neither do I. I'm hoping Joe will be back from his
mission so we can go out again tonight. We had such a
good time last night. He's really beginning to loosen up
now. He even kissed me last night without me having to
kiss him first."

Polly started pegging the wet clothes to the line.
"You really like him, then?"

Sadie smiled. "He's a really nice boy. Got really nice manners, too. Knows how to treat a lady, he does."

"But what about when he goes back to America? Aren't you going to miss him?"

"Well, of course I am." Sadie stuck a peg between her teeth and hooked another one over the line. "That's why I won't let myself get too fond of him. He's not really my type, anyhow. He's just fun to be with, that's all." She looked at Polly over the line of washing. "Don't worry, Pol. It's not like it was with you and Sam. It's not going to break my heart when Joe goes back."

Polly felt a pang at the mention of Sam's name. "I still miss him sometimes," she said wistfully. "I know one thing: I'll never get that silly over another Yank. I don't even want to go out with another Yank. I'll be sticking to the English from now on."

"Like the boy you're writing to in Italy?" Sadie grinned. "When's he coming home, then?"

"I dunno. He'd be going home to Surrey, anyway. That's where he lives."

Sadie shook her head. "You do pick 'em. That's miles away, near London. How're you going to see him if he lives all that way away?"

That was something Polly didn't want to think about right then. "It's a lot closer than America," she pointed out.

"Yes, but—"

Deciding she'd had enough of the subject, Polly interrupted her. "What if Ma sees all this washing on the line? She'll wonder where it came from. What am I going to tell her? What's going to happen when Lady Elizabeth goes looking for her clean knickers? What's Violet going to say if she finds you missing all day?"

"Would you stop worrying!" Sadie stuck another peg on the knickers on the line. "In the first place, think about when our drawers got stolen—it was daytime, wasn't it? He didn't take them at night."

"Yes, but—"

"If he doesn't come by the time your mum wakes up, we'll take them all off the line and I'll take them back to the manor. Then we'll try again tomorrow, all right?"

It sounded all right, Polly had to admit. Even so, she couldn't help the niggling feeling deep in her stomach that they were asking for trouble. Somehow, whenever she did things like this with Sadie, something always went wrong. She just hoped that this time, something would go right.

CHAPTER
❀ 9 ❀

"How long are we supposed to be out here anyway?" Clara whined, wrapping her cardigan closer around her thin body. "My boys will be wanting their dinner before too long."

"It won't hurt them to wait a bit." Marge lifted the field glasses and peered through them. She could see nothing but a flat ocean and a sky studded with puffy clouds. No dark shadows beneath the surface that might suggest an enemy submarine. No pinpoints of light twinkling signals to someone onshore. It was all so bloody boring.

"I don't know if they will wait," Clara grumbled. She leaned back on the hard park bench and stretched out her legs in front of her. "They're growing lads, you know."

Marge lowered the field glasses. "They're always eating, your boys. I don't know how you manage it with everything on ration like it is."

"I fill 'em up with bread and potatoes. At least we can get plenty of that." Clara held out her hand. "Want me to look for a bit?"

"Nah. There's nothing out there. I don't know why Rita's so blinking anxious to have us sit out here all morning. If anything's coming in from the beach they're not going to do it in daylight, now are they?"

Clara shrugged her shoulders. "Dunno. They might, if they want to get across the sand without stepping on a mine."

"Well, all I can say is, if I were a German, I'd wait until it was dark and take my chances with the mines."

"Seeing as how the rag and bone man got shot in the head by a German, I'd say they're already here."

Marge's stomach did a somersault. "Gawd almighty, I never thought of that. All Rita said was that there might be a spy in the village."

"There could be a whole lot of them. A whole bloody German battalion. How the 'eck would we know if they came in the middle of the night? There's no one out here to watch for them at night. No one wants to leave their children alone at night to watch for Germans."

Marge's heart started banging away like a big bass drum as Clara began wailing in a high-pitched voice, "What'll we do if they're here already? We can't fight them all by ourselves. They'll take us away and put us in one of them terrible prison camps!"

Already Marge could envision them all starving and freezing to death, staring through the wire fences at the guards pointing guns at them. The picture made her feel faint. Determined not to let Clara know how frightened she was, she said stoutly, "Of course we can't fight them on our own. That's what the army's for, silly. We'll just ring the army base in Beerstowe from the post office and tell them where they are."

"But we don't know where they are!" Clara wailed even louder.

"Well, we'll just have to find them then."

"The American base is closer," Clara said, visibly shivering now. "We could get the Yanks to come. They've got guns, too. They'd get here quicker."

"We'll ring them both," Marge assured her. "And the constables. But first we have to find them."

"Where could they be? Do you think they're hiding in the woods?"

"They might be." Marge frowned. The idea of traipsing through the woods looking for Germans who could jump out on them any moment or even shoot them was not her idea of a fun afternoon. A thought struck her and she brightened. "You know what? I think they'd hide in the old windmill. They could keep watch from the windows at the top and they'd have shelter at night if it rained." The more she thought about it, the more feasible it seemed. "Yes, that's where they'd be. I think we should look there first."

Clara didn't seem at all enthusiastic about the idea. "Why don't we just tell the constables where we think they are? Then they can call in the army."

"Don't be daft." Marge shook her head in disgust. "We're going to look right ninnies, aren't we, if we call in the army and there's no one there. First we have to go up there and make sure they're there, then we can go back to the village and raise merry hell."

"I don't think—," Clara began, but Marge, who was impatient to get it over with and get back home where it was safe, wouldn't let her finish.

"We're going," she said firmly. "It won't take that long to walk out there and take a peek at the windmill."

"It's an awfully long way back," Clara muttered. "'Specially if we have to run all the way."

Marge crossed her arms across her chest and glared at her friend. "Do you want to win this war or not? How are we going to save the village if we sit on our backsides and do nothing? That's what we joined the House-wives League for, wasn't it? To protect the village?"

"Actually I joined it for the knitting parties," Clara mumbled.

Marge let out her breath in disgust. "Come on. Let's get one over on Rita. She'll never forgive us if we manage to get a whole battalion of Germans captured. We'll probably be in all the newspapers and on the wireless news."

Clara's eyes widened. "You really think so? Rita will be so cross."

"Green with bloody envy, that's what she'll be." Marge grinned. "I can't wait to see her face when she finds out." She pushed herself to her feet. "Come on, let's go and find those Nazis before someone else gets there first. This is one war effort we're going to do all by ourselves."

Having sent Polly out to collect the rents, Elizabeth had the office to herself that morning. She found it impossible to concentrate on anything, however. A considerable portion of her mind was engaged in the hope that Earl would call, even though he'd warned her that it could be some time before he could contact her again.

Rather than sit there in what she knew was hopeless

futility, she decided to call on Bob Redding. In spite of the favorable opinions she'd heard about the man, she wanted to satisfy herself that he hadn't taken a gun and ended the life of the man who had more or less killed his daughter.

Her conviction that Clyde Morgan was murdered had grown stronger, fueled more by a hunch than anything else. Still, there was a familiar feeling niggling at her brain that told her she was missing something somewhere, and until she discovered what it was, she was compelled to search every avenue open to her. Bob Redding was at the top of the list.

She gave Alfie a ring, and learned that the Reddings lived in one of the cottages down by the bay. Apparently Mr. Redding had been a fisherman before he was called to duty, and no doubt planned on continuing his profession when he returned from the war for good, God willing.

She was halfway down the stairs when the bell clanged, announcing a visitor. Expecting Martin to materialize, she continued down at a leisurely pace, until it dawned on her that Martin wasn't there to open the door.

It didn't appear as if Violet planned on opening it either, probably because she expected Sadie to attend to it. Since there was no sign of the housemaid, Elizabeth had to assume she was somewhere at the other end of the mansion, probably cleaning up after the departure of the American officers.

There was nothing for it but to open the door herself. It took her a few moments to tug back the bolts and latches that held the massive door in place, during which the bell clanged loudly twice, nearly deafening her. As usual, she inwardly cursed the process, vowing as she always did to replace all those bolts and latches with a modern lock and electric bell.

Finally she slid the last bolt back and dragged the door open, breathing a little hard with the exertion. No wonder Martin took forever to open the door, she thought, then stared in shock as she recognized the visitor.

The object of her recent thoughts smiled back at her. "Good morning, madam. I do appreciate your taking the time and trouble to open the door for me. Your pleasant demeanor is a vast improvement over Violet's sour face and caustic tone, I can assure you." Martin doffed the trilby he wore and swept it in front of him with a deep bow. "I am forever in your debt."

Elizabeth's first thought was that her butler had been imbibing spirits of some sort. Her relief at seeing him made her voice sharp. "Martin, where on earth have you been?"

Martin blinked at her over the top of his glasses. The half dozen hairs on his head, disturbed by the removal of his hat, stood on end, waving in the breeze. There was something different about him, Elizabeth thought, though she couldn't put her finger on it.

Maybe he was standing a little straighter than usual, his eyes brighter than usual . . . something. The obvious answer that sprang to mind was the raffle ticket lady, Beatrice whatever-her-name-was. "Martin, have you been visiting your raffle lady friend?"

She watched with fascination as a curtain seemed to descend over her butler's face. His eyes took on a vacant stare and his voice sounded frail when he answered. "Raffle lady?"

"Yes. Beatrice somebody or other. She visits the

manor quite frequently, ostensibly to sell raffle tickets, though I suspect her main objective is to socialize with you."

A flicker of interest flashed across his face, then was gone. "Socialize?"

"You know what I mean, Martin. And do come in. I really don't want to have this discussion on the doorstep."

Martin carefully wiped first one shoe then the other on the mat at his feet before stepping over the threshold. Elizabeth closed the door, then turned to find him shuffling away from her at top speed, which for Martin was little more than the pace of a frightened worm.

"Martin! I'm not finished speaking to you!"

Elizabeth's voice echoed sharply across the hall and Martin halted, swaying rather precariously on his bowed legs. It took him several seconds to shuffle around to face her, by which time Elizabeth was quite sure he was deliberately emphasizing his fragility.

"I know it's none of my business," she said, as he stood blinking at her over his spectacles, "and you are perfectly entitled to your privacy. When you resort to staying out all night, however, I have to question the wisdom of your behavior. Violet and I feel a certain responsibility for your welfare, and it's not very considerate of you to worry us like this without some sort of explanation."

He stared at her for a moment or two, then said abruptly, "I was stargazing."

It was the last thing Elizabeth expected to hear. "I beg your pardon?"

"Stargazing, madam. You know, looking at the stars. I've taken up an interest in astronomy."

Certain he was pulling her leg, Elizabeth said dryly, "Really. Astronomy."

"Yes, madam. Quite fascinating, actually."

"I can imagine. Tell me, Martin, are you engaged in this new endeavor alone, or do you have company when you are staring at the stars?"

"Quite alone, madam."

"I see." Elizabeth pursed her lips. "And you feel compelled to do this all night long?"

"That is when you have the very best view."

"No doubt." Elizabeth walked up to him until she was almost toe to toe. "Martin, I do not believe one word you say. You're up to something, and I mean to find out what it is."

"Yes, madam. May I be excused now? I am rather fatigued."

He did look awfully tired, Elizabeth thought with another rush of concern. "Go and lie down," she ordered, "but first let Violet know you're back. I don't want her getting in a state worrying about you all day."

"Very well, madam. Good day to you."

A thought occurred to her and she called out after him. "Have you had breakfast?"

"Yes, madam, thank you. I had a plate of sausage, bacon, eggs, mushrooms, fried potatoes, fried tomatoes, and fried bread. Very tasty." He was moving away from her as he spoke, and his last words were barely audible, but she caught them. "A vast improvement over Violet's stodgy porridge, I can assure you."

She stared after him. Where in the world did he get a breakfast like that? If he was stargazing, as he maintained—and she had serious doubts about that—it had to be from a most unusual viewpoint indeed.

This wasn't the time to pursue it, however, and she had other matters to attend to for the moment. Later, she promised herself, she would corner her butler and demand to know where he had spent the last two nights, and why he was going to such great pains to hide where he had been.

The wind had picked up considerably by the time she rode her motorcycle along the narrow road that separated the harbor from the tiny shops that had once catered to the summer visitors. Most of the shops were closed and shuttered now, since very few people ventured far from home these days.

She found the cottage nestled on a steep slope, its leaded-pane windows almost hidden beneath its thatched roof. Parking her motorcycle, she was careful to turn the wheels into the grass verge.

An attractive woman answered her knock, and immediately gasped in surprise. "Lady Elizabeth! Whatever are you doing here?" She slapped a hand over her mouth. "That wasn't very polite, was it? I'm just so surprised to see you, that's all. I've seen your picture in the paper and seen you about town, but I never thought I'd actually get a visit from you."

"It's quite all right." Elizabeth smiled at her. "In the old days one would drop off a calling card announcing an impending visit. In my opinion the old customs were a good deal more civilized than the modern manners of today, and should be resurrected for the most part. I apologize for calling on you like this, but I would like a word with your husband, if I may?"

"Oh, Mr. Redding's not here, your ladyship,"—she opened the door wider—"but he should be home soon if you'd care to come in and wait. He's just gone down to the harbor to help his friend unload his catch for the day."

Elizabeth stepped inside the immaculate front room, and looked around with pleasure. Bright yellow cushions with white daisy appliqués decorated the brown sofa and armchairs, giving a splash of color to the room. Yellow and white checkered curtains hung at the windows, and a vase of daisies sat in the middle of the highly polished dining table.

"How refreshing," Elizabeth exclaimed. "I love daisies; they always seem to be smiling somehow."

Mrs. Redding's laughter echoed across the room. "I know what you mean. If you'll care to sit down, I'll put the kettle on."

"Oh, please don't bother." Elizabeth sat down on a comfortable armchair and removed her scarf. "I'd like to talk to you if you don't mind, Mrs. Redding."

"Not at all, and please, call me Marion. Everybody does."

"Thank you." Elizabeth paused, then added carefully, "I was so very sorry to hear about your daughter's tragedy. What a terrible accident that was."

Marion Redding's face clouded. "Indeed it was. Sheila is our only child, and I didn't think Bob was ever going to get over what happened to her. Not that one ever really gets over something like that, but we've managed to come to terms with it, and that's the best we can hope for."

"I suppose there's no hope that your daughter will recover?"

"None at all." Marion Redding sank onto the sofa, her hands clasped together. "Sheila will spend the rest of her life in a wheelchair, however long that may be.

She doesn't know anything that's going on around her. It's like she's asleep all the time, except her eyes are open. Sometimes she cries, but no one knows why, and it's so sad to see her like that."

"It must be very hard for you and your husband," Elizabeth said quietly. "I suppose you've heard that Clyde Morgan, the man responsible, has passed away?"

Marion nodded. "We heard he'd shot himself. Bob said he was probably eaten up with guilt for what he did and couldn't live with it anymore."

"And what do you think?"

The other woman sighed. "I really don't know, your ladyship. It's been more than two years, after all, and Clyde Morgan didn't strike me as the kind of man who would wallow in guilt over something that was an accident, no matter how badly it turned out."

A harsh voice came from the doorway, making them both jump. "What difference does it make? The miserable bugger's dead, and that's true justice."

Elizabeth stared at the man who'd just entered the room. He wore a dark sweater and a cloth cap, and a cigarette dangled from the corner of his mouth. He needed a shave and shadows underlined his dark eyes. His scowl drew his thick brows together and in one hand he held an axe, making him all the more intimidating.

"For heaven's sake, Bob!" Marion uttered a nervous laugh and got up from the sofa. "That's no way to greet the lady of the manor. This is Lady Elizabeth Hartleigh Compton. She wants to talk to you."

Bob Redding appeared unaffected by this announcement, though he did remove his cap. Very deliberately, he closed the door with an ominous thud. "Something I can do for you, your ladyship?"

Feeling somewhat unsettled by this bear of a man, Elizabeth said quietly, "I'm pleased to meet you, Mr. Redding. I do trust you are recovering from your injuries?"

He came farther into the room, his face a mask of indifference. "As well as can be expected, I suppose."

"He's expecting to go back to his unit in a week or two," Marion said hurriedly. "Aren't you, Bob?"

Her husband didn't answer, but kept his gaze on Elizabeth's face, his eyes narrowed and wary.

"Well, I won't keep you long." Elizabeth met his gaze steadily. "I just dropped by to let you know about the sudden death of Clyde Morgan. Your wife tells me you've already heard about it."

Not a flicker of expression changed in the man's gray eyes. "Yes, we did. Can't say I'm sorry." He ignored his wife's gasp of dismay. "As far as I'm concerned, the skunk got what he deserved."

"I can understand your bitterness, Mr. Redding." Feeling at a distinct disadvantage, Elizabeth got to her feet. "I imagine most people would feel the same way in your shoes."

"That's not to say I killed him."

Marion uttered another distressed cry. "I'm sure her ladyship didn't mean—"

"Oh, I think she did," Bob Redding said, his voice harsh and threatening. "Isn't that why you're here, your ladyship? To accuse me of murdering Clyde Morgan?"

CHAPTER
❄10❄

"For heaven's sake, Clara! Get a move on, will you?" Marge stopped for the umpteenth time and waited for her friend to catch up with her.

Panting and puffing, Clara trudged down the lane toward her, her face red and sweaty. "I'm hot," she announced unnecessarily as she drew even with Marge.

"One minute you're freezing, the next you're roasting." Marge jabbed a finger in her direction. "Take off your cardigan, you twit. No wonder you're so hot."

"I feel the cold." Clara swept a critical gaze up and down Marge's body. "I don't have no fat to keep me warm, like some people."

Marge bristled at that. "Hey, are you saying I'm fat?"

All the fight went out of Clara. "No, silly, of course not. I'm just tired, that's all. Let's forget about the Germans and go home."

"Forget about the Germans!" Marge's voice was shrill with disbelief. "Are you daft? We came all this way, didn't we? What if the place is running alive with Nazis? If we don't warn the village, they could be all over us by tonight."

Clara's face lost its ruddy glow. "Well, if there *are* Germans in the windmill, you've probably warned them by now. It's right over there, behind you."

Marge swung around. "Gawd, I didn't realize we were that close." She lowered her voice to a hoarse whisper. "We'd better duck down out of sight."

Clara immediately dropped to a crouch. "How are we going to sneak up there without them seeing us? There's no trees around here to hide us."

"There's trees on the other side of it. We'll work our way around and come in from that side."

"I still think we should have gone to the police station for help."

"We'll go when we're sure they're there," Marge insisted. "Come on, let's go."

"I can't walk like this." Clara stuck her foot out and tried to waddle forward in the crouch.

Marge muffled a giggle. "You look like a crab."

Clara shot to her feet. "I'm going home."

Grabbing her arm, Marge said quickly, "I'm sorry, I didn't mean it. Look, let's just walk normal until we get past the windmill. Even if they see us, they won't know we're looking for them. They'll just think we're out for a stroll. Then, once we get past them, we can duck back."

"What if they shoot us while we're going past?"

Marge hadn't thought of that. She felt a sudden urge to pee. "Don't be silly," she said, more in an effort to convince herself than anything. "Of course they're not going to shoot us. They don't want everyone to know where they are, do they? How are they going to take everyone by surprise if we all know they're there?"

Clara didn't look too sure of herself, but she trotted along by Marge's side, looking as if she were ready to bolt at the slightest sound.

Marge wasn't about to admit that her heart was pounding hard enough to come right through her chest by the time they'd reached the far side of the windmill. Any minute she'd expected to hear a bullet or two whine over her head, and it was a bit of an anticlimax when all remained quiet and peaceful.

For several minutes they stood there, waiting to get their breath back while they stared at the rickety wooden walls of the dilapidated windmill. No branches stirred in the midday sun. No birds twittered, no squirrels chattered, no inquisitive field mouse or rabbit rustled through the tall grass. Nothing but a tall, dark, forbidding windmill with silent sails and darkened windows. It seemed as if everything were waiting for something to happen. Something bad.

Marge shivered as the creepy feeling crawled down her back. "I don't like this. It's too quiet. Like someone's in there, watching us."

Clara uttered a whimper of fright. "I want to go home. *Now.*"

She started to walk away, but Marge grabbed a stretchy sleeve of her cardigan and dragged her to a stop. "Wait a minute! Let's just take a quick peek and then we'll get out of here. I swear."

"I'm not going in there!"

Clara's wail sounded loud in the hushed silence of the woods and Marge winced. "All right then. You wait here and I'll go. Then if they shoot me, you can run back and tell George and Sid that you let me go in there alone and now I'm dead."

Tears formed in Clara's eyes, but to Marge's relief, she stammered, "All right, then. I'm coming in there with you. But if I get shot I'll never forgive you."

"If you get shot, silly," Marge said grimly, "you won't be around to forgive me, so what's it matter? If you hear the slightest sound, you run like hell. Got it?"

Clara nodded, her eyes wide with fright.

Marge wasn't feeling too chipper herself, but she'd come this far and she wasn't about to turn back without taking a quick look inside that windmill. A large part of the force driving her was the anticipation of seeing Rita's smug face turn sour when she found out they'd helped catch a bunch of Germans.

Armed with this vision, she crept forward, bending over as low as she could before the fleshy folds of her stomach got in the way. Although their footsteps made no sound on the soft grass, she could hear her friend right behind her. Clara's teeth were chattering so loudly it was a wonder they didn't fall out.

They reached the door without seeing or hearing any movement from inside the dark, towering building. Very carefully, Marge pushed the door open. A loud creak made her jump nearly out of her skin. Clara muffled a shriek and Marge shot a warning look at her, her finger over her lips.

Braced to flee at the slightest provocation, she took one step inside, then two. It smelled musty and damp, and there was another odor she didn't want to analyze. A narrow beam of sunlight, with specks of dust swirling and dancing in its glow, slashed through the darkness from the high window above. The floor was uneven, with several of the floorboards missing or broken. Blinking to adjust to the shadows, Marge took a quick look around. Nothing. They were alone.

Clara crept up beside her and put her mouth to Marge's ear. "I can't hear nothing."

Her hair tickled Marge's nose and she backed away, fiercely shaking her head and pointing to the floor above them. There was another floor where somebody could hide, though if the Germans were up there, there wasn't room for more than a half dozen or so. That made her feel a little better.

The two of them stood absolutely still, barely breathing, while the silence thickened about them. Then Clara spoke in her normal voice, spiking Marge's nerves.

"There's no one up there. Let's go home."

"Shh!" Marge hissed at her, then froze as a sharp snap sounded overhead.

All color drained from Clara's face. "What's that?"

Marge swallowed. "Could be old wood. You know how it creaks. Or maybe a rat."

Clara squealed. "I hate rats."

So did Marge. What's more, her body ached with tension, and her chest hurt from not breathing deeply enough. "All right," she murmured, "let's go home."

Clara had turned toward the door and Marge had taken one step when the unimaginable happened. Above their heads they heard a distinct sound—*a loud and explosive sneeze.*

Marge stared at Clara, who stared right back at her, with eyes almost popping out of her head. Then, without a word, she bolted out the door with Marge hot on her heels, and they didn't stop running until they were all the way down the lane and back on the coast road.

Elizabeth did her best to ignore the axe in Bob Redding's hand as she faced him across the room. "I'm not here to accuse anyone, Mr. Redding," she said quietly. "But I would like to know why you think I would accuse someone of murdering Clyde Morgan, when the police are convinced it was suicide."

Bob Redding turned back to the door and leaned the axe against the doorjamb. When he faced them again, his expression had softened considerably. "Beg your pardon, your ladyship. I was a bit ahead of you, that's all. My mind gets a little blurry when that . . . when I hear the name Morgan."

"He didn't mean no harm—," Marion began, then subsided into silence when her husband shot her a vicious glare.

"I don't know if Morgan died by his own hand or someone else's," Bob Redding went on, "but I do know I weren't the only one to hold a grudge against him. I heard somewhere that the gun was in his right hand. Everyone that knew Morgan knows he was left-handed. He couldn't see out of his right eye, and he was always saying how lucky it was he was left-handed."

"He could have shot himself that way out of spite," Marion said, braving her husband's scowl. "You know, just to make the constables think it was someone else that killed him."

Bob uttered a scornful grunt. "He weren't that clever."

Marion stared at her husband in bewilderment. "But you said you thought he did it because of the guilt."

He nodded. "That's right, I did. But that was before I heard about the gun being in the wrong hand. The more I thought about it, the more I changed my mind. Morgan wasn't the kind who'd do himself in."

"Well, it couldn't be you, anyway," Marion said, glancing at Elizabeth as if to convince her. "You weren't even here the night Clyde Morgan died. You were visiting Sheila at the sanitarium in North Horsham, weren't you, Bob?"

Bob sent his wife a strange look that Elizabeth couldn't interpret. "I reckon I had as good a reason as anyone to want him dead," he said slowly, "but there are plenty of others. Ned Widdicombe, for instance."

Marion gasped and shot another scared look at Elizabeth. "I don't think Ned would . . ." Her voice trailed off as once more Bob glared at her.

"Who is Ned Widdicombe?" Elizabeth asked gently.

"He's a butcher, lives in North Horsham." Bob waved a hand at the chair Elizabeth had just vacated. "Sit down, your ladyship, and make yourself comfortable. I'll tell you all about Ned Widdicombe."

Reluctantly, Elizabeth lowered herself onto the chair. This big man made her uncomfortable, though if asked she'd be hard-pressed to explain why. Maybe it was the secret signals he was exchanging with his wife, or the evil look in his eyes whenever he mentioned Clyde Morgan's name. Whatever it was, she sensed an undercurrent of tension beneath the affable expression he now presented to her.

"Ned's mother used to live two doors away from us, in that little green house with the white fence." Bob walked over to a vacant chair and sat down. Holding his cap between his knees, he paused, as if sorting out what to say next. Finally, he went on, "Not long ago, Morgan came down here collecting, as he called it. If you ask me, it was no better than begging."

He ignored Marion's small sound of protest. "Anyway, my dear wife gave away some of my clothes to him, and books I hadn't read yet—"

"You'd had those books for years and never read them," Marion protested.

Ignoring her, Bob went on, "And a lot of other things she had no business giving away. Morgan must have thought he was on to a good thing. He went down to all the cottages looking for more bounty. That's when he met Mrs. Widdicombe. Widow she were, must have been in her eighties."

"Eighty-four, she were," Marion confirmed, then squirmed after yet another nasty look from her husband.

"Anyway, Morgan goes inside, picks up just about everything he could lay his hands on, and carts it off to sell it all. By the time Ned heard about it, the lot had gone. Morgan told him the old lady said to help himself to what he wanted, so he did. Ned was spitting mad. They had to hold him off Morgan, so I heard. Kept yelling at him that he'd pay him back for what he did."

"I see." Elizabeth shook her head. "What a dreadful thing to do."

"What's even worse," Bob said, "it was such a shock for the old girl, she dropped dead. Marion used to pop in there every day just to keep an eye on her, since Ned could only get down on Sundays, and she found her dead on the floor. Doctor said it was her heart and the shock of losing all her belongings."

"Ever so sad, it was," Marion chimed in. "Such a shock to find her like that."

"Anyhow," Bob said, getting to his feet, "if anyone had good reason to bump off Clyde Morgan, I'd say it were Ned Widdicombe."

Elizabeth got up, too. "Well, perhaps I'll have a word with Mr. Widdicombe."

"He's got a shop in the High Street," Bob told her. "You can't miss it. Widdicombe the Butcher's. Got a big sign in front of it." He opened the door, as if anxious to be rid of his visitor. "Thank you for calling on us, your ladyship."

Elizabeth nodded at Marion, then moved to the door. "Thank you for your time. I hope you are soon fully recovered, and I wish you all the best of luck when you go back."

For the first time, Bob Redding's eyes softened. "Very nice of you, Lady Elizabeth. Much obliged, I'm sure."

Elizabeth walked slowly down the garden path, fighting the urge to look back to see if Bob Redding was watching her. She had the feeling his eyes followed her until she had started her motorcycle and had ridden down the lane and out of sight.

"Do you think you'll go back to America with Joe?" Polly asked, leaning her elbows on the sink to get a better view of the back garden.

Sadie uttered a scornful laugh. "What, me? Go to America? What the heck would I do in America? Full of cowboys and Indians, it is."

Polly shot her a look over her shoulder. "Don't be daft, Sadie. That's only in the films. America has enormous wide roads and lots of cars, and big buildings and lovely houses with swimming pools. I've seen pictures of them."

"What, in *Photoplay*? What makes you think they're real? It's a film magazine, isn't it?"

"What about the cities like New York, that you see in the films, then? They're just like London. What about the pictures of the film stars' homes? They've got to live somewhere, haven't they? Are you going to sit there and tell me the beaches in Los Angeles aren't real? I didn't see no cowboys and Indians running around shooting arrers there."

Sadie grinned at her friend. "Okay, okay, don't get your knickers in a twist. I was just having you on, that's all. 'Course I know there's no cowboys and Indians in Los Angeles or New York, but I bet you anything they have 'em in Wyoming, where Lady Elizabeth's major lives."

Polly stared at her. "How d'you know where he lives?"

"I heard them talking." Sadie stretched her spine against the back of the hard chair. "He was telling her he goes riding on horses there. Miles and miles of open land, he told her. You can ride all day there and not see another soul."

Polly turned her back on the window and gazed dreamily at Sadie. "Ooh, how romantic. Can't you just imagine her ladyship riding on the back of his horse, hanging on to his waist?" She sighed, slapped a hand over her heart, and rolled her eyes at the ceiling.

Sadie burst out laughing. "She's more likely to be riding on her motorcycle chasing after him."

Polly's romantic visions vanished. "Well, I think she's madly in love with him, and I think he loves her, as well, so there."

"I hope not." Sadie's face sobered. "If you're right,

I can see trouble ahead for them. What's going to happen when he goes back to America?"

"She'll go with him, of course."

"Oh? Then what's going to happen to all of us, might I ask? What about Violet and Martin, and you and me? What about the Manor House? Who's going to take care of that?"

Polly stuck out her bottom lip. She didn't want to think about what might happen. Thinking of her ladyship and Major Monroe together made her feel warm inside, and she didn't want anything to spoil that. Why did things always have to be so blinking complicated?

With her mood dampened, she turned back to the window. The sun shone directly in her face, momentarily blinding her. She blinked . . . and blinked again. No, she wasn't seeing things. She let out a yell that echoed all the way up the stairs. "Sadie! The knickers! They're gorn!"

Sadie got up so fast she knocked over the chair. She swore, then picked it up, muttering, "You'd better be joking." Thrusting Polly aside, she stared out of the window.

There was the sound of a door opening and Polly's mother's voice floated down the stairs. "Polly? Is that you? Why aren't you at work? What are you doing down there?"

Polly grabbed Sadie's arm. "Come on," she whispered hoarsely. "He can't have got far. Let's go after him."

"You were supposed to be watching for him," Sadie began, then yelped as Polly dragged her across the kitchen. Footsteps started down the stairs, and Edna, Polly's mother, called out, "Polly? What are you *doing*?"

Polly didn't wait to answer her. She shoved Sadie through the back door and out into the garden. Side by side they raced for the gate and threw it open. They were just in time to see a bicycle disappear around the bend.

"Come on!" Sadie yelled. "After the bugger!"

Polly threw herself on her bicycle and pedaled like mad down the road after Sadie, who was already speeding away from her. They rounded the bend and there in the distance was a very short man huddled over the handlebars of his bicycle as he raced along the coast road.

Sadie waved a frantic arm at Polly and yelled, "Get a move on, Polly! We can't lose him now!"

Polly put her head down. She didn't know where they were going, or what they would do if they caught up with the thief. They had reached the top of the hill and were gathering breakneck speed, and all she cared about now was staying on her bicycle.

CHAPTER

❈ 11 ❈

Marge thought she was going to die by the time she and Clara stumbled down the High Street, both of them limping and sobbing for breath. Clara hadn't said one word to her since they left the windmill, and Marge was thankful for that. She wouldn't have been able to answer her anyway.

At long last the police station came into view, which was just as well, since she and Clara were attracting a good deal of attention as they lurched down the street. Marge shot a glance at her friend. Clara's hair was all over her face, which was as red as a beetroot and covered in sweat. Daft thing still hadn't taken her cardigan off. No wonder she was dripping.

The steps were almost too much for Marge, and by the time she actually got to the door she had to lean on it to push it open. Clara stood at the bottom of the steps, holding her sides and making horrible noises like a cow in heat.

Marge left her there and staggered into the office, where she thankfully fell onto the chair. She'd sat on that chair a few times in the past, but it had never felt as comfortable as it did right then.

George, she noticed, sat behind his desk, one hand holding a half-eaten Banbury cake halfway to his mouth, which was stuck wide open. She waved a hand at him to go on eating, while she fought to get enough air back in her lungs to speak.

George looked from her to his hand, hesitated, then shrugged and thrust the cake in his mouth.

"Germans!" Marge managed to gasp when she finally found her voice.

George dropped the remaining piece of cake onto his desk. Making a tsking noise with his tongue, he picked up the cake, dusted it off on his jacket, and shoved it in his mouth.

Momentarily distracted, Marge gazed at the smear of sugared crumbs on George's uniform and wondered what the inspector would say if he saw that.

"I beg your pardon?" George said, his voice muffled by the food in his mouth.

Marge pulled in some more air, then coughed. There was always a faint odor of horse manure in the police station. She'd forgotten not to breathe through her nose. She opened her mouth, pulled in more air, then shouted, "Germans!"

George raised his eyebrows. "Where?"

Marge waved a hand at the door. "At the windmill! Dozens of 'em!"

George swallowed, and immediately choked. Coughing and spluttering, he pulled a huge white handkerchief from his trouser pocket and wiped his eyes.

The respite had given Marge time to get her own breath back. "Clara and I went up to look and they're there, all right."

George started to speak, coughed again, then said hoarsely, "You saw them? Did you see their uniforms? Did they have tanks? Guns?"

Marge's stomach turned over in fright. Until that moment it hadn't seemed real, more like a film she was acting in, but now it all seemed dreadfully, frightfully real. "We heard them," she said, her voice dropping to a whisper. "They were hiding up on the second floor but we heard them. Clara and me bolted out of there. We didn't see no tanks, but—"

At that moment the door burst open. Marge screamed, while George leapt to his feet, his eyes looking ready to bulge right out of his head.

Clara fell through the doorway and landed on her knees. "I don't feel well," she moaned.

Marge patted her chest as her heart resumed beating. "Gawd, Clara. You gave us such a fright."

George cleared his throat and sat down again. "Now then," he said, in his pompous policeman's voice, "let's have the story from the beginning."

"We don't have time to tell the story!" Marge shouted, heaving herself to her feet. "You've got to ring the army, haven't you. If we don't get them first they'll be all over the village. Heaven knows how many of them are hiding in the woods." She caught her breath. "That's probably where they've hidden the tanks!"

Looking startled, George dragged his gaze from Marge to Clara. "Did you see these Germans, too?"

Clara opened her mouth, but before she could say anything, Marge yelled impatiently, "Of course she did!

Ring the blinking army before we all get captured and sent to them dreadful prison camps."

Clara started crying. "I don't want to go to prison! I want to go *ho-o-ome*!"

"Now look what you've done!" Marge rushed over to Clara and helped her up. "If you don't ring the army right this minute I'm going to tell everyone it's your fault Sitting Marsh is in the hands of the Germans. I wouldn't be surprised if Adolf hisself walks down the High Street before too long."

George reached for the telephone. "All right, all right. Just pipe down while I ring the army."

"Ring the Yanks!" Clara said, apparently having recovered from her fright. "They'll be here quicker."

"Ring them both!" Marge started for the door, dragging Clara with her. "I'm going home to lock all my doors and windows. I'm not having no bloody Nazis poking around my belongings."

Outside in the fresh air, she pulled in a deep breath. She'd done her duty. Now it was up to George and Sid to take care of things. Feeling proud of her contribution to the war effort, she started down the steps on wobbly knees. Just wait until Rita Crumm heard about this one.

It took Elizabeth the best part of an hour to ride to North Horsham and find the butcher's shop. The rumbling in her stomach reminded her it had been several hours since she'd eaten breakfast and she promised herself that as soon as she'd talked to Ned Widdicombe, she'd have a spot of lunch at the fish and chip shop next door.

There were no customers in the butcher's shop, which was really not surprising, considering the hour.

The housewives typically shopped first thing in the morning, queuing for whatever meager cuts of meat they could get on their weekly ration books. By noon they were back home preparing the midday meal.

It occurred to Elizabeth then that Violet was expecting her for lunch and was probably tearing her hair out wondering where she was and when she was coming home. Poor Violet. What with worrying about Martin's mysterious nightly jaunts and now Elizabeth's absence for lunch, it was no wonder the housekeeper was a little testy at times.

She'd take something home for tea, Elizabeth decided, as she spotted a bakery across the street. She had her coupon book with her, and at the very least, could buy a nice fresh loaf of bread, since bread wasn't on ration.

Reaching the door of the butcher's shop, she pushed it open and, to the tune of a tinkling bell, stepped inside. The smell of raw meat and sawdust was unpleasant, and she held her breath for a moment. There was no one behind the counter, and since the door was unlocked, she assumed the butcher had retreated to a back room.

She had hardly formed that opinion when a man emerged from a hallway at the back of the shop. Short in stature, his vast circumference made him look as wide as he was tall. He was clad in a white coat and a blue and white striped apron liberally smeared with blood.

In spite of her need to question the man, Elizabeth felt a strong urge to excuse herself and leave. A butcher's shop always made her uneasy. Seeing all those dead carcasses hanging from hooks was unsettling, and the lethal-looking knives and choppers on the blood-soaked chopping board weren't exactly reassuring, either.

The butcher stood in the shadows, as if reluctant to come forward. Obviously he resented being disturbed during his midday break. "What can I do for you?" he asked gruffly. "I don't have much left this late in the day."

Elizabeth let out her breath in a rush. "Oh, a pound of sausages, if you have them, please."

The butcher grunted and moved over to the chopping block where strings of sausages hung in long strands. He reached up, took down a strand, chopped off a string of sausages, and threw them on the scales.

Elizabeth made herself move deeper into the frigid shop. "I was talking to Bob Redding this morning," she said brightly. "I understand his wife was a very good friend of your late mother."

The butcher turned to look at her and now she could see his face quite clearly. His beady little eyes were almost buried in layers of fat, and a nasty-looking scar divided one eyebrow and sliced down most of his cheek. "What's it to you?" he said rudely.

Elizabeth wasn't used to being spoken to in that deplorable manner. She drew herself up straight and said haughtily, "As lady of the manor in Sitting Marsh, it is my duty to protect and care for the villagers. Had I been aware that your elderly mother lived alone, I would have made it my business to look in on her now and then. I feel somewhat responsible for what happened when Clyde Morgan paid her a visit, and I regret that the unfortunate incident caused her death. I thought you might like to know that Mr. Morgan has now passed away."

"So I heard." Apparently unfazed by the presence of

his illustrious visitor, Ned Widdicombe weighed the sausages, cut half of one off the end of the string, then wrapped the rest in white paper.

Elizabeth handed over her ration book and a half crown and waited for her change. "I'm sure that must bring some comfort to you," she said when he handed her the coins and her ration book. "I can understand how you must have felt, losing your mother that way."

The beady eyes narrowed. "I heard he shot himself."

"Well, that was the assumption at first." She decided to stretch the truth a bit. "There has been a development, however, that leads the constables to believe someone may have murdered Mr. Morgan."

Ned Widdicombe moved back to the chopping block, picked up the remaining sausages, and strung them up with the others. "Good riddance, that's what I say," he muttered.

Realizing she was getting nowhere, Elizabeth said boldly, "I imagine the inspector will be questioning those people who might be able to shed light on the murder."

Now she had the butcher's full attention. He stared at her for several uncomfortable moments, then said sharply, "What's that got to do with me?"

"Motive," Elizabeth said quietly. "Your mother's death was hastened by Mr. Morgan's actions, was it not? I think that's a strong motive for murder, don't you?"

The butcher continued to stare at her in silence for another long moment, then startled her by erupting into hoarse laughter. "My mother was eighty-four years old," he said when his irreverent mirth had subsided.

"She was on her last legs as it were. Besides, all that happened weeks ago. If I was going to do the miserable bugger in, I would have done it before now."

She'd heard that somewhere before, Elizabeth vaguely remembered. "Sometimes one has to wait for the right circumstances," she murmured.

"Oh, you an expert on murdering, then?"

She smiled, though it was the last thing she felt like doing. "As a matter of fact, I am."

The butcher dug his fists into the mounds of fat around his waist. "Well, your ladyship, for your information, I was here in the shop the night Morgan died. Doing my accounting, if you must know."

Elizabeth carefully put away the ration book in her handbag and slipped the coins into her small purse. "I don't remember mentioning that Mr. Morgan had died during the night," she murmured.

"It were in the newspaper, weren't it."

"Were you alone when you were doing the accounting?"

"No, I weren't. My wife was with me, wasn't she. She'll tell you. So you can stop your bloody snooping and get out of my shop." He paused, then added with a decided sneer, *"Your ladyship."*

It was definitely time to go. Without a word, she twisted around and stalked out of the shop.

She dearly would have loved to speak to Mrs. Widdicombe, but apart from the fact that she had no idea where to find her, and it was doubtful the sinister butcher would have enlightened her, there was no doubt in her mind that the woman would vouch for her husband, whether or not she was with him that night. Ned

Widdicombe was a particularly nasty specimen, and seemed quite capable of terrorizing his wife into submission.

Seated by the window in the sparse eating area of the fish and chip shop a few minutes later, she spotted the butcher leaving his shop, locking the door behind him before hurrying off down the street. No doubt he was on his way to warn his wife to confirm his alibi in case of further questioning. Just as well she hadn't sought out Mrs. Widdicombe. She had no wish to encounter that man again.

Although her appetite had been somewhat tempered by the disturbing exchange, Elizabeth managed to enjoy a plate of cod and chips lathered with malt vinegar and sprinkled generously with salt, a thick slice of bread and butter, and two pickled onions, washed down with a cup of piping hot tea. Absolutely delightful.

Feeling invigorated by the meal, she left the shop and climbed aboard her motorcycle. There was plenty of time before she needed to be back in the village, she decided. There was one more stop she'd like to make before returning home.

There was only one sanitarium in North Horsham, so it took no more than a few minutes to locate it on the outskirts of town. Surrounded by trees, the imposing dark brick building looked rather intimidating as Elizabeth paused at the heavy wrought-iron gates. At least this was one gate that hadn't been melted down to make airplanes, she thought wryly.

After ringing the bell, she gave her name to the uniformed nurse who hurried down to greet her. Leaving her motorcycle parked outside, she followed the nurse up the long driveway to a wide flight of steps leading to massive doors.

Another bell summoned someone else from inside, and the drawing of heavy bolts reminded Elizabeth of her own front door. She half expected to see Martin standing there as the door opened, but she was greeted instead by a fresh-faced young woman in a nurse's uniform.

Both women seemed impressed by her presence, and, her dignity restored, Elizabeth asked to see Sheila Redding, explaining she was a friend of the family.

The nurse who had opened the door accompanied her down a long corridor, where elderly people sat huddled in chairs or wandered aimlessly about with vacant expressions.

Elizabeth's heart ached for them all, and she was even more determined to never let Martin wither away in such a lonely, desolate place, even if he did insist on disappearing every night.

The friendly nurse asked lots of questions about the Manor House and Elizabeth's duties in the village. She seemed fascinated by the idea of a woman being in such a distinguished position, and quite heartened by the fact that the villagers accepted Elizabeth as their guardian and provider.

"It's not often you see a woman in a position of power," she remarked as she paused at the door of a room with wide barred windows. "I always say women can be just as strong and intelligent as men, if not more so. I think we should have a woman for a prime minister, after Winnie goes, of course. Fat chance of that, though."

"I quite agree," Elizabeth said as the nurse opened

the door. "Most women would agree with you, but just try convincing the men of that."

The nurse smiled. "That's the whole problem, isn't it? They think of us as the weaker sex, and think the only thing we're good for is cooking meals and taking care of babies. The war's changed all that though, m'm. I think the men are in for a big shock when they come back from the war. Women aren't the same as they were when the men went away. They've had to stand on their own two feet, and they like it."

"Indeed. I understand there are far more women working full-time jobs now than ever before."

"We've had to, haven't we." She ushered Elizabeth into the room and closed the door behind her. "Not enough men to do it, that's for sure. The women have taken over, and they're not going to give that up just because their hubbies are coming home."

Elizabeth felt a familiar pang of misgiving. The war had indeed changed things. No matter how much people wanted things to go back to the way they were before, that was extremely unlikely. She couldn't help wondering how they would all adapt to this brave new world that was emerging.

She followed the nurse across the room, past smiling, nodding patients who either played board games at small tables or sat knitting or reading in comfortable chairs. These people seemed happier than those in the hallways, and Elizabeth felt a little better, until she saw the young girl seated in a wheelchair.

She sat by the window that overlooked the grounds, her body so still it was hard to tell she was alive. Her eyes were open, though vacant, as Elizabeth approached.

"Can she understand if I speak to her?" Elizabeth asked, reaching out to touch a motionless hand.

"Hard to tell." The nurse gently leaned the girl forward and plumped up the pillow at her back. "Sometimes I think she can. Now and then I see a tiny movement of her lips, as if she's trying to smile. Sometimes she cries. No one knows why."

"How sad." Elizabeth felt like crying herself. "It must be dreadful to sit here day after day, without hope of a normal future."

"Oh, there's always hope," the nurse said quickly. "Scientists are working hard all the time to find out why the brain shuts down like this but leaves the body working just fine. Sheila breathes on her own, and the doctors think she could move her arms and legs and even learn to walk again if she really wanted to, but they don't know how to make her want to try. They just keep moving everything for her and hoping that one day she'll want to try it on her own."

"Well, I certainly hope that happens soon," Elizabeth said, giving the girl's hand a gentle pat. "A young life is such a terrible thing to waste. I wonder if she recognizes her father when he comes to visit. It must be heart-breaking for him to see her like this."

"Oh, she hasn't seen her father since it happened." The nurse patted the pillow in place.

Elizabeth stared at her. "But surely you must be mistaken. I was talking to him just this morning. His wife mentioned he was here last Monday."

The nurse looked puzzled. "He's home? I thought he was fighting somewhere abroad. I keep records of all the visitors that come in here, your ladyship.

Everyone has to sign in the register, just like you did. I can assure you, Mr. Redding hasn't set foot in this sanitarium since his daughter was admitted two years ago."

CHAPTER

❈ 12 ❈

Pumping wildly to keep up with Sadie, Polly started getting nervous when she realized the thief was heading away from the village and out into the country lanes. The mad chase had already led them through the High Street at heart-stopping speed. Sadie had barely missed a frightened housewife who just happened to be crossing the street with her shopping bags, and Polly had almost fallen off her bicycle when a large dog bounded in front of her wheel.

As they'd toiled up yet another hill behind the fleeing figure, Sadie waved an encouraging arm at Polly, both of them too breathless to speak. Now they were racing along the downs, heading in the direction of the Manor House.

Before they got close, however, the thief veered off the coast road and plunged into a lane. Sadie, who had shortened the distance behind him, overshot the opening and had to brake. Polly caught up with her as she turned into the lane.

Her breath came out in painful gasps but she managed to form a few words. "Where—the heck—is he—going?"

Sadie shrugged, shook her head, then took off after him. Polly pulled in a resigned breath, then started after her. It was more difficult to see the rider ahead of them now. The lane curved and twisted through trees and high hedges, and even Sadie disappeared from Polly's view now and then.

She hurtled around a bend, intent on catching up with her friend, but then swerved as Sadie suddenly appeared in front of her, standing astride her bicycle with an odd look on her face.

Going too fast to stop, Polly crashed into the hedge. Her bicycle twisted away from under her, and she landed on her elbow in a prickly bush. "Ow!" she yelled, and then let out a muffled protest as Sadie clapped a hand over her mouth.

"Shush! He'll hear you!" she whispered fiercely. Slowly she took her hand away from Polly's mouth and whispered, "He's on the other side of the hedge."

"What's he doing?" Polly mouthed, her sore elbow forgotten.

Sadie shook her head and lifted her shoulders. Placing a finger over her lips, she crept down the hedge to where it joined up to a gate. Moving an inch at a time, she poked her head around the bushy shrub.

Polly held her breath, then let it out in a rush when Sadie straightened up.

"He's flipping gone!" Sadie hung over the gate, looking right and left. "I don't believe it. Where'd he go?"

Polly groaned. "There go my knickers. Don't tell me we went through all that for nothing."

"He can't have got far or we'd see him. He must be hiding somewhere." She pointed with her finger. "Over there. I bet he's in the windmill."

Polly got up gingerly and brushed bits of leaves and twigs off her skirt. Joining Sadie at the gate, she peered over it at the weathered building across the field. "Are you sure?"

"It's the only place he could be. He couldn't have reached the trees on the other side before I looked over, so he must be in the windmill."

"Maybe he'll leave the knickers there and go off somewhere," Polly said hopefully. "After all, he can't live there, can he. He must live somewhere else. Why didn't he take them home with him?"

"Coz he knows we was following him, silly. He's waiting to see what we do next."

Polly hadn't thought of that. "So what are we going to do now?"

"Go in after him, of course, and get our knickers back."

"What if he's waiting in there with a knife or something?" She shuddered at the thought. "You said we would just go back and tell George we know where he is."

"I know I did," Sadie said heavily, "but by the time George gets back here the thief won't be here anymore, will he. And we don't know who he is or where he lives, so there's not much point in telling George about him, is there."

"I suppose not." Polly shivered, in spite of the sticky warmth of the afternoon.

"Besides, he's not very big, is he. The two of us should be able to manage him."

"I don't like the idea of going in there after him, though. It's so creepy in there. There's rats and spiders and everything."

"Don't be such a baby." Sadie squared her shoulders. "All right, we'll leave the bicycles here and we'll cut around through the trees to the other side. That way he might not see us coming."

"But what if he does?"

"Look, like I said, there's only one of him and two of us." Sadie propped her bicycle up against the gate. "He'll probably run when he sees us coming, and then we can just go in there and get our knickers."

"I'm not so sure about that." Polly dragged her bicycle up on its wheels, gave it a quick examination to make sure it wasn't damaged, then leaned it against the gate next to Sadie's. "All right, let's get this over with. But I'm taking a big stick in with me."

"Good idea." Sadie set off for the trees. "We'll pick one up in the woods."

A few minutes later, each armed with a thick branch from a stout elm, the two of them crept up to the door of the windmill. Sadie signaled to Polly to stay behind her as she pushed the door open and looked in. After a nerve-shattering moment, she beckoned to Polly to follow and stepped inside.

Polly crept in behind her, sheltered behind Sadie's sturdy body. All was quiet within, and after a moment, Polly peered around Sadie's arm. "There's no one here," she whispered.

Sadie pointed to the floor. "Someone's been here. Look at all the footsteps in the dust."

"Looks like they've been and gone." Dropping her

stick, Polly came out from behind Sadie and stared around. "Now how are we going to get our knickers back?"

The answer came from an unexpected place—right above her head. She heard a smothered giggle, followed by a chorus of shushes.

Polly looked at Sadie, who stared back at her, her face turning red with temper.

Throwing back her head, Sadie yelled, "You'd better bleeding get down here right this minute, or I'll light this match in my hand and burn this place down with you inside it."

A scuffling answered her threat, then hushed voices conferred with each other.

"I'm counting to ten!" Sadie yelled. "One . . . two . . ."

"All right, all right," a voice called out. "We're coming."

A pair of legs, bared from the knees down and ending in scruffy socks and shoes, descended the creaking stairs from the upper floor. The owner of the legs turned out to be a boy about ten years old, with huge freckles all over his face and a missing front tooth.

He landed with a thump on the floor, due to the three missing steps at the bottom. Behind him tumbled three more boys, one behind the other, none of them older than the first.

Sadie waited for them, one hand on her hip, stick held high, eyes blazing. She made a formidable figure, Polly thought with admiration as her friend pointed the stick at the boys and said in a voice of doom, "You'd better tell me what you're doing up there, and I want the truth. If I find out you're lying you'll all go to jail until you're twenty-one years old. Your mothers are not going to like that."

At the mention of their mothers, the boys exchanged nervous glances. "Don't hit us, miss! We didn't mean no harm," the first boy said quickly. "It was a quest, see?"

Lowering the stick, Sadie frowned. "Whatcha mean, a quest?"

"Well," another boy piped up, "we have a secret club, and you can't be a member until you've brought back a dozen pairs of ladies' knickers."

Nervous giggles from the boys greeted this announcement.

In spite of her outrage, Polly felt a tug at her lips and quickly straightened her face. "How many of you are in this club?" she demanded.

"Nine," the first boy announced. "But me and Timmy are the leaders. The rest are just members. They're not all here now. Just the ones what had to get the knickers today."

"So you're the one who told the others to steal the . . . unmentionables," Sadie said, frowning at the boy.

"Yes, miss. We was going to bring them all back, though. Honest!"

"How do you know which ones are which?" Sadie glared at them, looking even more menacing. "How many people did you steal from?"

The boys exchanged nervous glances. "About six or seven," one of them admitted.

The smallest of the group, a pudgy little boy with short hair that stuck up all over his head, said proudly, "I got mine from the Manor House!"

"Did you now." Sadie dropped her stick on the ground

and crossed her arms. "Just how did you get them down from the line, might I ask?"

"I knocked them off with the prop." His smug expression faltered a little. "They got a bit dirty. They might need another wash."

"I'll wash you, you little . . ."

Sadie stepped toward him and he backed away, his face crumpling with threatened tears.

"Wait," Polly said quickly. "Where are all the knickers now?"

This time there was no giggling at the forbidden word. "Up there." The first boy pointed with his finger.

"What's your name, son?" Sadie demanded.

"Jimmy, miss."

"Well, Jimmy, you get back up them stairs and fetch down all them knickers this instant. All of them. You hear me?"

"Yes, miss. Hold on, I won't be a minute." He scrambled back up the rickety steps so fast he lost his footing on one of the gaps and stuck his foot through the hole.

Polly held her breath as he dragged it free and climbed on up out of sight. "Those stairs aren't safe," she told the other boys. "You could fall down and be killed. Promise me you won't go up there again."

"But it's our meeting place!" one of them wailed.

"Polly's right," Sadie said forcefully. "You've all got to promise not to go up there again. Find another meeting place. There's plenty of places around. What about that old barn on Miller's farm? He never uses it. Ask him if you can meet in there. I bet he won't mind."

"And no more stealing knickers," Polly added, wagging her finger at them. "You'll have to think of a different quest. All right?"

A chorus of "Yes, miss!" answered her, just as Jimmy appeared on the stairs, his arms full of underwear.

"Throw them down," Sadie ordered, and the boy let them drop. Some fell with a plop, while the rest fluttered down in a colorful lacy waterfall of silk.

Polly started gathering them up. "We're going to need some help carrying these back to the bicycles," she muttered. "I just hope we can get them all in the baskets."

"We'll cram them in somehow." Sadie started picking up the rest of the garments. "Here, you boys, help me pick these up. You can carry them back to the gate for us before you go home."

The boys obediently pounced on the knickers, which were looking decidedly worse for wear. Sadie waited until the last pair was picked up, then ordered the boys to form a line.

Clutching the underwear to their chests, the boys marched out of the door with Sadie and Polly bringing up the rear.

They were halfway across the field when a sudden shout brought the boys to a halt. Sadie almost fell over them, and Polly stopped dead, unable to believe what she was seeing.

All along the hedges, in front of the gate, all the way around the windmill on either side were men in uniform, all of them carrying rifles pointed ominously in their direction.

"Blimey," Sadie said, her voice hushed with shock. "It looks like the whole bleeding army's out there."

Arriving back at the Reddings' cottage, Elizabeth was greatly relieved to find Marion alone. The questions she

needed to ask would be more easily delivered without
Bob Redding's fierce glare to intimidate her.

Obviously surprised to see her renowned visitor twice
in one day, Marion invited her in, and Elizabeth wasted
no time in coming to the point.

"I've just returned from North Horsham," she told
the flustered woman, after refusing her offer of a cup of
tea. "I went there to speak to Ned Widdicombe."

"Ah, yes, the butcher." Marion sat on the very edge
of her couch, her hands twisting in her lap. "Did you
find the shop all right?"

"Yes, I did." Elizabeth laid her purse on her lap. "Not
a very sociable man. Rather rude, I thought."

"He can be very blunt," Marion agreed. Her gaze
shifted to a clock on the sideboard, and Elizabeth wondered if she was expecting her husband home.

"While I was there, I thought I'd stop by and pay a
visit to your daughter."

Marion's gaze jerked back to Elizabeth's face.
"Sheila? You went to see her?"

Elizabeth leaned forward. "Mrs. Redding, why did
you lie about your husband's whereabouts on Monday
night? He wasn't in North Horsham, was he? The nurse
told me he hasn't visited his daughter since she was admitted to the sanitarium more than two years ago."

Marion's face crumpled. "I know it was silly of me,
but I was so afraid . . ." She sniffed, and hunted for a
handkerchief in her apron pocket. "Bob was gone until
late that night. He said he was helping a mate of his repair
his boat and they had a drink or two together afterwards,
but when I heard about Clyde Morgan I thought . . ." Her
voice trailed off and she blew her nose hard.

"You thought he might have killed Clyde Morgan,"

Elizabeth said gently. "So you decided to give him an alibi."

Marion nodded. "He was ever so cross with me after you left. He said as how I didn't trust him, and that he was telling the truth, and that I could talk to Evan and he'd tell me Bob was there all the time until he came home." She blew her nose again. "That's his friend's name, Evan Darby. He's a fisherman. Lives just down the road."

"I see." Elizabeth sat up. "Have you had a chance to talk to Evan yet?"

"No, but I talked to his wife, Janet, a little while ago. She told me the two men were working in the boatyard until it got dark, then they both came up to the house and shared a couple of beers." Marion sniffed. "I should have asked her before, I suppose. It would have saved all that time worrying. I suppose I was scared to ask her, in case Bob was lying and he really did shoot that poor man." Her eyes were wet with tears when she looked at Elizabeth. "I should have trusted him, Lady Elizabeth. I should have known he couldn't have done something that dreadful."

Elizabeth got to her feet. "Well, I can understand why you were concerned. Your husband certainly had good reason to hate Mr. Morgan. I'm just glad we could clear the matter up like this. It must be a great relief for you."

Marion rose, blowing her nose once more. "What about Ned Widdicombe?" she asked. "Did he have anything to say about the murder?"

"He certainly didn't seem to be upset about it." Elizabeth walked to the door. "As for him being involved in some way, that's highly unlikely. He told me he was working on his accounts with his wife on Monday night."

In the act of opening the door, Marion paused and

stared at her. "His *wife*? Ned Widdicombe doesn't have a wife. He used to have one years ago, from what Bob told me, but she ran off with someone else and Ned's never looked at another woman since."

Elizabeth stared back at her. "Are you sure? Perhaps he got married again."

Marion shook her head. "Well, he hadn't up until last week, your ladyship. He was here sorting out his mother's things in the old cottage. Him and Bob are on really friendly terms. I'm sure he would have mentioned a wife if he'd got married recently."

"Well," Elizabeth said, stepping out into the late-afternoon sunshine, "that's very interesting. Thank you, Mrs. Redding. You've been most helpful and I sincerely hope that your daughter's health improves in the near future."

"I don't think that's going to happen," Marion Redding said sadly. "But thank you for the thought. Children are so precious, aren't they? I worried so much about Sheila when she was growing up. I never let her out of my sight. When this happened I blamed myself, thinking I should have been able to prevent it. But no matter how hard you try, you can't control your child's life, or what happens to them. You can only pray that things will turn out right for them."

Elizabeth's heart ached for the woman as she walked back down the immaculate garden path to her motorcycle. How sad. Sheila obviously had been loved and well cared for, and now this tragedy had robbed her parents of so much. They would never see their child become a productive adult. Nor would they see her married, and giving them grandchildren. They would miss so much because of a senseless accident. Marion was right. Parents can't control what happens to a child, no matter how protective they may be.

Sitting astride her motorcycle, she felt an odd pang of recognition. It was a familiar sensation—her brain trying to tell her something important that she couldn't quite recognize. Something she knew that could shed light on the mystery of Clyde Morgan's death.

As she roared down to the High Street, she tried to remember everything that she'd heard that day. Was it the fact that Ned Widdicombe had lied about his alibi? Was Marion telling the truth about her husband's whereabouts the night Clyde Morgan died? Or was there something else, something she'd stored away without realizing its importance at the time?

Whatever it was, it was going to drive her crazy until she could grasp it and bring it out into the light. Because, more often than not, whenever she felt this particular sensation, she had the answer she was seeking, and the solution to the puzzle.

CHAPTER
❀ 13 ❀

Frozen to the spot, Polly could only stare at the menacing ring of armed men. Even the young boys seemed too shocked to move, and only Sadie appeared capable of saying anything.

"What are all these GIs doing out here?" she muttered as a tall soldier detached himself from the line and marched purposefully toward them.

A thin voice piped up from one of the boys. "Are they going to shoot us, miss?"

"Not if I can help it." Sadie stepped in front of the boys and bravely faced the oncoming officer, much to Polly's admiration.

The American paused a few feet in front of her, his gaze moving slowly down to the pile of underwear clutched in Sadie's arms. "What the—?" His gaze shot up to her face. "Just what in hell are you all doing here?"

Sadie's face turned red, and she shoved the knickers

behind her back, causing most of them to flutter to the ground.

More washing, Polly thought mournfully. At this rate, they'd be standing at the sink all day long.

"We thought someone had been stealing washing off the lines," Sadie said quickly, "but it was all a big mistake."

"I'll say it was a mistake." The officer's astonished gaze swept over the boys and their bundles, then to Polly, who was beginning to wish she could sink through the ground, and finally to the pile of drawers on the ground. "What were you planning to do with all of this?"

"Take it back where it belongs." Sadie gave him an uncertain smile. "The lads just borrowed it for a while, that's all. No harm in that, is there?"

The officer's face remained stiff and uncompromising, but there was a twinkle in his blue eyes when he murmured, "I reckon it all depends on whether or not you're an owner of those . . . ah, clothes."

"Yes, sir," Sadie said heartily. "That's what I say. This is something we should definitely sort out ourselves."

The American shaded his eyes and peered past her at the windmill. "Did you happen to see anyone else in there?"

"No, sir." Sadie looked back at the boys, who answered in chorus.

"No, sir! No one, sir!"

"There weren't no one in there but the lads," Sadie assured him. "Why? Are you looking for someone?"

The officer shook his head. "Never mind." He glanced at the boys again then back at Sadie. "I take it those are your bikes behind the shrubs?"

Sadie nodded. "We were just on our way home, weren't we, Pol?"

Polly nodded, still too embarrassed to speak.

The officer turned and signaled with a wave of his arm. Four GIs detached themselves from the line and came forward at a trot.

"Brent, Adams, take a look in there, just in case," the officer ordered.

The two men jogged toward the windmill, rifles in hand. One of the remaining soldiers, a dark-eyed young man with an engaging grin, winked at Polly behind the officer's back.

"You two escort the young ladies back to their bicycles," the officer ordered. "Help them carry all this stuff. As for you boys, I suggest you all get back home before I decide to slap you all in jail."

The boys needed no further excuse. They dropped their armloads of knickers on the ground and took off faster than a hare at the races.

Unable to meet the good-looking GI's amused gaze, Polly trailed behind Sadie and the soldiers as they carried the underwear back to the gate. They were greeted by whistles and catcalls from the line of soldiers, who were now grinning and waving at their comrades marching toward them with their arms full of ladies' knickers.

Polly was sure she'd never be able to look another American in the eye as the GI stuffed her basket full of the embarrassing underwear.

Sadie appeared to have no such qualms. She helped the other GI load up her basket, chatting happily about Joe and asking if they knew each other.

On the other side of the hedge, the officer had restored order, and all was quiet as they waited for their companions to return from the windmill.

"There you go, sweetheart," the Yank said as he tucked the last pair into Polly's basket.

"I'm not your sweetheart," Polly mumbled.

"So what's your name, then?"

Without looking at him, she muttered, "Polly."

"Polly who?"

This brought her chin up. The GI was smiling at her, and in spite of her determination to ignore him, her stomach flipped. He really was good looking. Almost as handsome as Sam.

Thinking of Sam hardened her resolve and she dropped her gaze again. "Polly Barnett. Not that it's any of your business."

To her immense discomfort, the GI leaned across her basket until his face was inches from hers. "What if I'd like to make it my business? What do you say to that?"

"I'd say you're out of luck."

This didn't seem to bother the GI at all. "My name's Warren, by the way," he said. "Warren Hudson. You can call me anything, though, just so long as you call me."

"I don't waste my time with Yanks," Polly said, just as the officer's voice cut across the hedge.

"Move it, you two!"

The tall American straightened. "Well," he said softly, "I guess I'll just have to change your mind about that, Polly Barnett." He turned to his companion and nudged him in the arm. "Come on, let's go."

Polly watched out of the corner of her eye as the two of them went through the gate and closed it behind them.

She was unprepared when Warren Hudson leaned back over and gave her another broad wink before disappearing from view.

"Looks like you got yourself a new boyfriend," Sadie said as the two of them mounted their bicycles.

Polly sniffed. "I told you, no more Yanks. One was enough for me. I'm not going through that again."

Sadie started pedaling down the lane, her laughter ringing out on the late-afternoon air. "I wish you could have seen your face when those GIs bent down to pick up all those knickers. Talk about beetroot cheeks! You looked as if you were on fire."

"Very funny." Polly pedaled so hard she rode right past Sadie. "Good job me mum couldn't see us standing there in front of all those Yanks with all those knickers in our arms. She'd have died of shame."

"Well, you'd better not tell her how many Yanks know what we're wearing under our skirts now."

Polly groaned and pedaled harder, anxious to be away from the scene of her humiliation and to be rid of the load of underwear under her nose.

"Bet you see that GI again!" Sadie called out from behind her.

Polly didn't answer, but she felt an uneasy quiver of apprehension at the thought. What if she did bump into him again? She wouldn't be able to look him in the face, that was for sure.

She shook her head, reminding herself again how much it hurt when Sam went back to America. No matter how good looking or exciting Warren Hudson might be, she was absolutely, definitely, positively not going to fall for a Yank again. So there.

• • •

On her way home Elizabeth decided to stop by Rose Clovell's house. Not that she suspected the poor woman of murdering Clyde Morgan, of course. Rose Clovell was a petite, nervous woman, the kind who would trap a spider and put it outside rather than kill it. No, it was more a need to explore every avenue, to convince herself she'd left no stone unturned.

She found Rose at home, tending to a clematis in her back garden. Laying down a pair of pruning shears, the frail woman greeted her guest with a wan smile. "I was wondering when you'd call on me, your ladyship," she said as she led Elizabeth into her tidy parlor. "I'd heard you were asking questions about the death of Clyde Morgan."

"Word does get around fast in the village," Elizabeth murmured as she took the seat Rose offered her.

"Yes, well, it's a small village, isn't it. Would you like a cup of tea?"

"Thank you, but I'm actually rather late for supper so I won't keep you long." Elizabeth waited while Rose shooed a large black cat off an armchair and seated herself.

The cat stalked off across the room, tail waving in indignation. Elizabeth watched it jump up on the window seat and begin delicately washing one elegant paw. Something hummed in her brain . . . the feeling she knew something . . . a cat and an armchair . . . What was her mind trying to tell her?

Rose spoke, making her jump. "What is it you want to know, Lady Elizabeth?"

Elizabeth brought her thoughts back to the matter at hand. "I happened to be passing by and thought I'd drop in and see if you are well. All this business with Clyde

Morgan must have brought back some unpleasant memories for you."

Rose nodded, her small teeth worrying at her bottom lip. "Well, yes, it did, actually. I'm really not surprised someone shot that man. No one liked him, you know."

"It really hasn't been decided if someone shot him." Elizabeth watched the other woman's face carefully. "It's more a theory of mine, that's all."

"Oh." Rose appeared to think about that. "Well, as I said, it wouldn't surprise me." She shot a look at Elizabeth. "You're wondering if I killed him, aren't you?"

Somewhat taken aback, Elizabeth started to deny it, but Rose cut her off.

"Oh, it's all right, your ladyship. I can see why you'd think that. After all, I blamed Clyde Morgan for the death of my son." She paused for a moment, then shook her head. "That was when it first happened, and I wasn't thinking straight. What happened to my boy was an accident, pure and simple. I know that now. My Arnie, he was a hooligan. Always in trouble. Always coming home covered in bruises . . . wouldn't tell me where he got them. He'd been fighting, of course. It was only a matter of time before he got into trouble."

Rose's voice faded away in Elizabeth's ears as the insistent buzz of recognition intensified. Something about bruises . . . Iris Morgan's boy . . . the cat . . .

It came to her all at once in a blinding flash. Of course. How terribly obtuse of her. How could she have missed something so significant?

"I'm sorry, Mrs. Clovell." She leapt to her feet, guiltily aware of Rose's startled expression. "I've just remembered something important and I simply must get back to the manor right away. Do forgive me."

"Of course." Rose scrambled to open the door for her, barely getting there ahead of her. "It was nice of you to drop by, your ladyship. I hope I might see you again in the future."

"Oh, of course!" Elizabeth stepped outside, waved a frantic farewell, and hurried down the path, no doubt leaving a befuddled Rose Clovell behind her.

She'd finally put it all together and she needed to talk to Iris Morgan right away. There was no time to go back to the manor now. Supper would have to wait until she'd taken care of this matter.

She fleetingly wondered if she should call George, then realized he would be home by now. The station would be closed. Besides, she needed to confirm her suspicions before she could make any firm accusations, and she was far more likely to get the answers she needed if she wasn't accompanied by a constable.

Seated astride her motorcycle, she bounced on the kick start and the engine roared to life. After tucking her scarf around her head, she tied it in a firm knot, then set off for the village.

Violet turned down the gas on the stove until the soup was at a low simmer. "We'll wait another fifteen minutes," she said, "then we'll eat without them."

Sadie sat alone at the kitchen table, impatiently staring at the clock. She wanted to get supper over with so she could keep an eye out for Joe. He'd told her he might be back that evening and she didn't want to miss him.

"I wonder where Lady Elizabeth is," she murmured as Violet sat down at the table. "It's not like her to be late for supper."

"Probably tearing around the countryside on that motorcycle of hers." Violet propped her elbows on the table and rested her chin on her hands. "What's worrying me more is where Martin has gone. This is the fourth night in a row he's disappeared."

Sadie looked at Violet in concern. The crotchety housekeeper never confided in her like this, and it bothered her. Violet had to be really worried about Martin for her to let her hair down like this. "Per'aps he's got a lady friend he's visiting and doesn't want you to know," she suggested.

"No doubt. The question is, what's a man his age doing out all night and how does he get where he's going?"

Sadie frowned. She couldn't quite see the old fogey on a bicycle. She knew he couldn't drive a motorcar and it was too far to walk to the bus stop. Martin got tired out walking up the stairs. "Per'aps someone's picking him up."

"That's what I think." Violet sighed. "But who? And where do they go?"

Sadie sat up straight. "What we have to do is follow him! Without him knowing, of course."

Violet lowered her hands. "I've already thought of that. The problem is, he slips out when I'm not looking."

Sadie reached out and patted Violet's arm. "You just leave it to me. I'm very good at following people, I am. I followed that little bugger today all the way to the windmill, didn't I?"

Violet gave her a sharp look. "You followed who?"

Sadie sighed. She and her big mouth. "We found the knickers thieves," she said, and proceeded to tell Violet the whole story.

Violet's face grew more and more disapproving,

especially when Sadie got to the part about the Americans seeing them with their arms full of underwear. "I just hope they didn't know you'd come from the Manor House," she said when Sadie was finished. "Most embarrassing for her ladyship."

"We never said a word about that," Sadie assured her. "Anyhow, as I was saying, I'm good at following people, so I'll watch Martin like a hawk tomorrow and I'll follow him to wherever he's going."

Violet seemed unconvinced. "You won't be able to follow a car if one picks him up."

"Watch me. I can go pretty fast on me bicycle. In any case, I can find out who it is picking him up. That'll be a start."

Pushing her chair back, Violet rose to her feet. "Well, if anyone asks, I know nothing about it. I'm not asking you to do anything, you understand. It's all on your shoulders."

Sadie nodded. "Mum's the word. Now how about dishing up that delicious soup before me belly button disappears into me back?"

"Enough of that, young lady," Violet snapped, returning to her usual crabby self, much to Sadie's relief. "I'll serve it up when I'm good and ready." She moved over to the stove, muttering, "Very inconsiderate of her ladyship, I must say. Not turning up for supper without a word to say she wasn't coming home."

"Maybe she went down the pub for a pint," Sadie said with a grin.

"And just maybe I'll wait another hour for her if you keep giving me lip." Violet glared at her. "Do you want your supper now or what?"

"Yes, please," Sadie said meekly. Violet was quite

capable of keeping her word, and Sadie was afraid if she hung around in the kitchen much longer, Joe would get back and she wouldn't be there to see him before he went to his quarters.

She ate the soup and chunks of bread and butter without another word, while Violet played around with hers until Sadie could have screamed with frustration. She couldn't leave the table until Violet had finished her supper, and the way things were going it looked as if she'd be there until midnight.

At long last Violet laid down her spoon, and Sadie was free to leave the room. Pulling off her apron, she charged up to her room and ran a comb through her hair. After adding a dash of lipstick and a touch of eau de cologne behind her ears, she opened her window and leaned out.

She could just see the edge of the courtyard from there, and sure enough the bonnet of a jeep poked out from the corner of the mansion. The Yanks were back.

Flying along the great hall, with its imposing portraits frowning disapproval at her, she sped toward the east wing and prayed she'd be in time to catch Joe. He didn't like her calling on him in his quarters. The other officers teased him and Joe wasn't very good at ignoring them. He was a really sensitive bloke and got embarrassed easily.

At first Sadie had taken it personally, thinking he was ashamed to let his mates know he was taking her out. After one memorable argument, however, she realized that it was just the way Joe was, and that it didn't take much to turn his face red and make his tongue trip over itself.

She often wondered why she bothered with him. He

was not at all like the blokes she usually fancied. Every time she saw him, though, she got a warm feeling inside. A comfortable feeling, knowing she didn't have to try to put on airs and graces or pretend to be someone she wasn't. Joe was a good friend, and she liked being with him. For now, that was enough.

She reached the stairs that led down to the courtyard just in time to see a group of officers trudging up them. The looks on their faces turned her stomach. She always knew when something had gone wrong with a mission. She could tell by the way they came up the stairs, none of them talking and poking fun at each other like they usually did.

For a moment fear crawled in her belly when she didn't see Joe right away. She was just about to ask someone, but then she saw him turn the corner in the flight of stairs, his head down, his shoulders hunched.

Relief chased away caution, and she called out to him, "Joe? You're all right, aren't you?"

The other officers passed with no more than a glance in her direction. No sly comments, no teasing remarks. She waited, heart beating anxiously, for Joe to climb to the top of the stairs.

When he reached her, he seemed to have trouble looking at her, glancing everywhere but at her face.

"What is it, Joe?" She grabbed hold of his arm, heedless of the sidelong glances from the two airmen coming up behind him. "What happened?"

Joe looked down at his shoes and mumbled, "We had a couple of gliders come in with us."

She stared at him in confusion. "Gliders?"

"Aircraft coming in without engines."

It took her a moment or two to make sense of what

he'd said. "You mean they had to land without an engine?"

"They made it back to base, but the kites broke up on landing. Major Monroe was in one of them."

Sadie's stomach dropped to her boots. "Oh, God. Is he . . . ?"

"I don't know." Joe's eyes were bloodshot when he finally looked at her. "They took him away in an ambulance. It didn't look good."

For a moment Sadie couldn't breathe. She lifted her chin and stared at the ornate ceiling above her head. "How in God's name am I supposed to tell that to Lady Elizabeth?"

CHAPTER

❀ 14 ❀

Iris wasn't home when Elizabeth arrived there a few minutes later. Tommy answered the door to her knock and gave her a sullen shake of his head when she asked for his mother.

"She's not come home from the village yet," he mumbled. "I don't know when she's coming home."

Elizabeth tried to soften his frown with a smile. "May I come in and wait for her?"

"Mum said we were not to let anyone in while she's gone." He started to close the door, but just then a loud wail from inside the house turned his head.

"That sounds as if your sister has hurt herself." Elizabeth pushed open the door again and purposefully stepped over the threshold.

Tommy looked as if he would try to stop her, but Katie wailed again and, giving up, he dashed up the hallway and disappeared through a door. Seconds later he reappeared, carrying a sobbing Katie in his arms.

"She fell and bumped her head," he muttered.

Leaving the door open, Elizabeth hurried forward. "Let me look." She followed Tommy into the parlor, where he sat the child down on the couch.

Elizabeth laid down her handbag and approached the child, who stared up at her with wet eyes and her small thumb stuck in her mouth.

Gently parting the blond hair, Elizabeth felt a small knot beginning to rise on the child's head. "Fetch me a flannel soaked in cold water," she ordered Tommy.

He hesitated for a moment, then fled into the kitchen.

"There, there, sweetheart," Elizabeth murmured, folding her arms around the sniveling child. "We'll soon make it all better."

Katie answered her by bursting into loud sobs. *"I want my mummy!"*

Tommy came back with a dripping facecloth and Elizabeth wrung it out over the hearth before applying it to the squirming Katie's head.

The child yelled at the contact, then sobbed while Elizabeth rocked her in her arms.

Gradually the sobs subsided, and Elizabeth met Tommy's anxious gaze. "She'll be all right," she assured him. "It's just a bump. It will stop hurting soon." She glanced more closely at his jaw. The bruises were now fading to an ugly yellow. "I hope your face has stopped hurting, as well."

Tommy snatched his gaze away from her and stared at his sister instead. "It's all right," he mumbled.

Elizabeth decided now was the time to test her theory. "Your mother said you'd been fighting that morning I was here, but that's not quite true, is it? Bruises take one or two days to turn that deep purple. Someone else hit you before that day, isn't that right?"

Tommy shook his head fiercely, pressed his lips together, and stared down at the floor.

"Tommy," Elizabeth said gently, "was it your father who hit you?"

The boy remained silent.

Elizabeth tried again. "It's all right, Tommy. No one is going to get into trouble as long as you tell the truth."

He looked at her then, and the look of dread on his face chilled her heart. "Mum said we were never to talk about my father again." His gaze shifted to a spot behind her, and his eyes widened.

With a jolt of apprehension, Elizabeth turned her head.

Iris stood in the doorway, her eyes blazing with suppressed fury. "Might I ask what you are doing here in my house, Lady Elizabeth?"

Katie wailed, struggled out of Elizabeth's arms, and ran to her mother, sobbing bitterly.

Iris stooped and gathered her up, then glared at Elizabeth as she slowly straightened.

"Katie fell and bumped her head." Tommy was in such a rush to explain, his words tumbled over each other. "The lady came in to help and she put a flannel on her head and she stopped crying and I was just—"

"Tommy!" Iris rapped out sharply. "That's enough. Take your sister to the bedroom and make sure she doesn't fall down again."

Katie wailed again and clung to her mother's neck. "Don't wanna go!"

Iris disentangled the child's arms and handed her

over to her brother. Katie's wails filled the house as Tommy carried her off, then they faded behind the door he closed behind them.

"I apologize, Mrs. Morgan," Elizabeth said, gathering up her handbag. "I came to see you, and Tommy opened the door just as Katie cried out. I only wanted to help, that's all."

Iris nodded stiffly and walked over to the couch, where she picked up the wet facecloth. "Thank you, your ladyship. What did you want to see me about?"

"I wanted to ask you . . ." Elizabeth paused, then took a deep breath. "I wanted to ask you if your husband physically abused your children."

Iris stared at her for a moment, then turned away. "If you're asking if he spanked them, well, yes, he did. Kids need discipline, you know."

"I'm asking if he abused them," Elizabeth said softly. "Those bruises on Tommy's jaw. They weren't caused by him fighting with other boys that morning. Those were days-old bruises. I suspect they were caused by his father."

Iris's bottom lip trembled, then she said sharply, "That's nonsense. Clyde was a strict father, but he wouldn't beat his children."

"I think he did, Mrs. Morgan." Elizabeth moved closer to her. "I think that's why Katie hits her teddy bear and shouts at it. She's copying her father. Clyde Morgan abused your children, didn't he? I think you were frightened for them. He had to be stopped, before he did them real harm."

"No!" Iris turned on her, eyes blazing. "You don't know anything! Clyde shot himself. I don't know why, but that's what happened. The constable said so. It's over and done with. My husband is dead. Why can't you just leave it at that and leave us alone!"

Elizabeth's glance strayed to the armchair in the corner of the room. "The first time I came here you mentioned you'd washed that chair."

Iris sent a wild look at the chair. "What's that got to do with anything?"

Elizabeth sighed. "Forgive me, Mrs. Morgan, but taking into account the general look of your house and garden, it seemed odd to me that you would go to the trouble of washing an armchair unless you had a specific reason."

Iris's gaze was steady when it met hers. And as cold as a winter's sea. "The cat pissed on it," she said bluntly.

For a long moment the two women stared at each other, then Elizabeth sighed again. "Well, I'll take my leave. I hope Katie's bump on the head gets better soon."

"I'll see you to the door."

Elizabeth stepped out into the hallway with Iris following close behind.

As she opened the door for Elizabeth, Iris said quietly, "My husband shot himself, Lady Elizabeth. For everyone's sake, let's leave it at that."

Bidding her good-bye, Elizabeth hurried down the path to her motorcycle. She was more certain than ever that Clyde Morgan had died in that house. Probably in the armchair that Iris had gone to all that trouble to wash. There didn't seem to be any way she could prove it, however.

The sun had dipped below the level of the trees as she roared up the hill toward the manor. Moths danced in the fading dusk, and an evening mist crept from the ocean across the sands. Usually this time of day gave Elizabeth a sense of peace, as if the countryside were getting ready to put away its cares and rest for the night until the dawn heralded a new day.

Tonight, however, she felt overwrought, her thoughts churning in a restless chaotic whirl that drained her mind. She put it down to the exchange she'd had with Iris Morgan. Her instincts insisted that Iris had killed her husband to protect her children, but without the proof she couldn't be certain of that.

Then again, she wasn't at all sure she'd be doing the right thing by hunting for the truth. What would happen to Tommy and Katie if Iris were imprisoned for killing her husband? All she could think about was Katie clinging to her mother's neck, sobbing.

How could she condemn a woman for going to such dreadful lengths to protect her children? After everything they'd suffered, wouldn't it be better for them to have at least one parent to love and take care of them in their own home?

To what kind of life would she be subjecting them if she was successful in sending their mother to prison? Could she honestly live with that on her conscience? What would be best for the children—to live with the woman who'd murdered their father through her love for them, or perhaps be separated and miserable in a strange home?

Wrestling with the problem gave her a headache. Feeling incredibly weary and out of sorts, she cruised up the driveway and into the courtyard.

The moment she turned the corner of the building she saw the jeeps and her heart sang. Her problems fading, she hastily wheeled her motorcycle into the stable then hurried around to the kitchen door. There was no time to wait for Martin to open the front door, assuming he was even there to open it. All she could think about now was seeing Earl again.

She burst into the kitchen, realizing as she did so that she was late for supper. Violet was at the sink, scrubbing violently at a pot with a stiff brush.

Surprised to see her housekeeper engaged in such a menial task, Elizabeth threw her handbag down on a chair, saying brightly, "Shouldn't Sadie be doing that?"

"She should," Violet said crisply, without turning around, "but she's off somewhere and I needed to keep my hands busy. You're late, by the way."

"I'm sorry." Elizabeth glanced at the clock on the mantelpiece. "I had to stop by . . . somewhere, and it took longer than I expected." She looked at the stove, where something that smelled very good simmered in a saucepan. "I'm hungry now, though."

"There's soup and there's bread." Violet tossed her head in the direction of the table. "Sit down and I'll get some for you."

Something in Violet's voice alerted Elizabeth. She sat down at the table and folded her hands. "Violet? Is something wrong?"

Violet threw the brush on the draining board with a loud clatter and turned to the stove. "Those blasted Germans," she muttered. "They've really gone and done it this time."

Elizabeth frowned. "Gone and done what?"

Violet turned to face her, and Elizabeth was alarmed to see her eyes swollen and red, as if she'd been crying. "They've got a new kind of bomb," she said, her voice trembling. "It's a terrible thing. It flies without a pilot, all by itself. Then, when it gets over London, the engine stops and the airplane falls to the ground and blows up."

"Oh, my," Elizabeth murmured, the cold feeling in her chest beginning to spread throughout her body. "How awful."

Violet sniffed, and cleared her throat. "They've already started sending them over. They're falling on London, flattening houses and blowing big holes in the streets. The explosions are terrible, so they say."

Elizabeth carefully watched her housekeeper's face. Something else was wrong. Something she didn't want to think about. A sort of premonition that had been simmering in her mind, like the soup on the stove, ever since she'd left Iris Morgan's house.

"Anyway," Violet went on, "the Americans have been going over to Germany and bombing the factories. Trying to stop them, they are. They're trying to shoot them down, too, but they say a lot of the buzz bombs will get through."

"Buzz bombs?"

"That's what they're calling them, because of the buzzing noise they make. They sound just like an angry swarm of bees, they say."

"How frightening."

"Yes, it is." Violet gulped. "Lizzie, your major went over there today."

Now she knew. She felt like crying but her eyes were dry. Her mind refused to believe what she knew she was about to hear. "What are you trying to tell me, Violet?"

"He made it back to base, Lizzie . . . but—" Her voice broke. "He crashed when he landed. They don't know . . . I don't know if he's . . ."

She had to be strong. She'd known all along this could

happen, and in some ways she'd been prepared for it. But oh, God, no one had told her how much it would hurt. No one had told her the pain could obliterate everything from her mind, except the realization of how much she might have lost.

"Where is he?" Her voice seemed unrecognizable, even to her.

"The hospital in North Horsham. Lizzie, I—"

"I'm going there." She surged to her feet, heedless of Violet's protests.

"You can't, Lizzie. You can't ride that motorcycle all that way in the dark. Wait until tomorrow. You'll have better news then."

Elizabeth headed for the door, afraid to trust her voice to answer Violet.

"You haven't had your dinner yet," Violet said, her voice rising. "Besides—"

Already halfway up the stairs, Elizabeth never heard the end of the sentence.

Outside in the cool night air, her mind cleared somewhat, and as she made her way around to the stable and passed the jeeps in the courtyard, she made a quick decision. Traveling by jeep would be faster and a good deal safer than the motorcycle in the dark.

She was tempted to try driving it herself, but soon dismissed that idea. After one memorable attempt to drive one of the jeeps, which had ended with her overturning the vehicle, she had avoided getting behind the wheel again, despite Earl's attempt to persuade her to allow him to teach her.

Earl. Hurrying up the back stairs to the east wing, she still couldn't grasp the fact that Earl was injured, possibly . . . No, she would not believe that. Until she actually saw for herself that all was lost, she would hang on to a shred of hope, and cling to that for now. She would not even think beyond that, because to do so was to look into the gates of hell.

As luck would have it, several of the officers were getting ready to depart as she arrived at their quarters. Despite all they had been through, and the fact that this might be the only respite they would get from the horrors for some time to come, to a man they enthusiastically volunteered to take her to North Horsham.

So adamant were they, that it took several tosses of a coin before two officers were elected to go, both of them assuring her they would much rather be visiting Major Monroe in North Horsham than getting drunk at the Arms.

Leading the two men down the stairs, Elizabeth found their clattering footsteps reassuring. She would not have wanted to make that journey alone, no matter how anxious she was to find out about Earl's condition.

She was even more gratified when the rest of the officers, instead of heading off in the opposite direction to the Tudor Arms, followed them all the way into North Horsham in a small convoy of jeeps.

Crowding into the admissions area of the large hospital, the men caused quite a commotion, until a stern sister in starched skirts arrived on the scene and sternly ordered them to be quiet or leave.

The men ushered Elizabeth forward, then stood silent as she asked the sister the fateful question. "I'm inquiring about Major Earl Monroe. I understand he was brought into this hospital sometime today."

The sister's face took on a grave expression that terrified Elizabeth. "He's in critical condition. The doctors are hopeful they can save him, but that's all I can tell you at the moment."

Weak with relief at the news he was still alive, Elizabeth said quickly, "I want to see him."

"I'm afraid he's not allowed visitors. He needs to rest." She took a watch from her pocket and looked at it. "If you'll excuse me . . ."

"I won't disturb him. I just—" Elizabeth paused, afraid her voice would betray her.

"He's heavily sedated," the sister said, looking impatient. "He won't know you're there."

One of the officers stepped forward, holding his cap in his hands. "This is Lady Elizabeth Hartleigh Compton," he said, his voice strident and formal. "She is responsible for Major Monroe's welfare. I must insist that you allow her into the major's room. He would want her there."

The sister looked from him back to Elizabeth. "Oh, I didn't realize . . . excuse me, your ladyship. Let me speak to the doctor and I'll let you know as soon as I get his permission."

"Thank you." Elizabeth watched her hurry off, then turned to the officer who had come so gallantly to her rescue. "That was very kind of you, Captain Crawford. I'm afraid I'm not thinking very clearly. While I'm about it, I'd like to thank you for bringing me here tonight." She looked around at the solemn faces surrounding her. "I'd like to thank all of you for coming."

"Sure, sure," the men murmured, looking embarrassed. "Anything for the major."

"Since the major can't have visitors," the captain said, gesturing at the door, "why don't you guys take off and find a bar somewhere? I'll stay with her ladyship until she's ready to go home. I'll catch you up on any news later. There's nothing you can do if you stay, anyway."

It took some persuading on the captain's part, but eventually the men reluctantly drifted off, leaving Elizabeth alone with him.

Seated in the quiet waiting room, she felt inordinately weary. Earl was alive for now, but she had no idea the extent of his injuries, or indeed, if he would pull through. She felt a tremendous sense of urgency, afraid that if she didn't see him soon, she could be too late. She couldn't bear the thought of never having the chance to say good-bye.

"Don't worry," Captain Crawford said quietly. "The major's a tough guy. He'll make it."

"I hope you're right." She gave him a wan smile. "This is very kind of you, Captain, but it really isn't necessary for you to sit with me. I feel guilty keeping you away from your friends."

The officer waved away her comments with an impatient hand. "Earl's a great guy. I'm sure every one of those guys would rather be here than passing the time in a bar."

Her throat threatened to close on her and she quickly swallowed. "Tell me about your home, Captain. You must have family waiting for you in America."

"I do, and if it's okay with you, your ladyship, I'd like it if you called me Duane."

This time her smile was wider. "Of course, Duane. Now tell me about your hometown."

For the next forty minutes she listened to Duane Crawford's account of his life in Texas, only half aware of what he said, her attention distracted by her gnawing worry about Earl.

If the captain noticed her inattentiveness, he was much too polite to show it, and she made a mental note to express her gratitude later, when she was more composed.

He was telling her about a parade that was held every July the Fourth in his hometown, and how he and his brother rode in a cart pulled by two horses, when he broke off abruptly in mid sentence.

Following his gaze, Elizabeth felt a leap of apprehension when she saw the sister heading toward them.

"Here comes the old battle-axe," Duane Crawford muttered. "Guess we'll find out now how bad Earl really is."

CHAPTER 15

"Madam has gone to North Horsham," Violet said as she put the last cup and saucer away in the kitchen cupboard. "I don't know when she'll be back."

Sadie glanced up at the clock. "It's almost ten o'clock. Did she take her motorcycle? How's she going to ride it in the dark?"

"Don't ask me. I'm only the housekeeper." Violet slammed the door shut.

"She must be so upset. She shouldn't be riding in that state—"

"It's not up to us to tell Madam what she should or shouldn't do."

"You do it all the time," Sadie pointed out.

"That's my business, not yours." Violet glared at her. "Why aren't you in bed, anyhow?"

Sadie plopped down on a chair next to the table. "Why aren't you? You're always in bed by this time."

"I'm waiting up for her ladyship." Violet started cleaning the stove with a dishrag.

"I cleaned that once already," Sadie commented.

"Well, I'm cleaning it again."

"All right, all right, keep your flipping hair on." Sadie propped an elbow on the table. "I came to tell her ladyship that Martin is home. I saw him come up the driveway."

Violet stopped cleaning and stared at her. "Walking?"

Sadie shook her head. "He got out of a posh black motorcar. Then it drove off. I couldn't see who was driving it. The moon wasn't bright enough that side of the house. I did see it ride over the flower bed as it went around the driveway, though. Desmond's going to throw a fit about that."

Violet came over to the table. "Never mind Desmond. How long ago was this?"

Sadie shrugged. "About half an hour ago, I suppose."

"Why didn't you come and tell me straight away? I could have asked Martin where he'd been. He's more than likely asleep by now."

"He wouldn't have told you if you'd asked him."

"He might have done if I'd told him you'd seen the motorcar."

"Well, it's too late now, ain't it."

"*Isn't* it." Violet turned back to the stove. "I'll have to ask him in the morning."

Sadie drew invisible patterns on the table with her finger. "Do you think the major's dead?" she asked abruptly.

Violet went very still, then said quietly, "I sincerely hope not, but if he is, well, that's war, isn't it."

Sadie felt a spurt of anger. "How can you say that?

Everyone knows her ladyship is bonkers over him. This will break her heart. I know how I felt about Joe when I thought he wasn't coming back, and I don't even love him."

Violet sent a sly look at her over her shoulder. "Don't you?"

Sadie stared at her. "Well, no . . . of course not . . . I mean . . ." She let her voice trail off. *Did she love him?* No, she couldn't. Joe was Joe . . . a nice chap, a good friend, that was all. "He's a friend, that's all," she repeated aloud, more to convince herself than Violet.

"I hope you mean that," Violet said, her back to Sadie once more. "Because if you don't, then you're in for a heartbreak every bit as painful as her ladyship's."

A cold feeling crept up from Sadie's stomach and settled in her chest. "I wouldn't fall for no Yank," she said roughly. "I'm not that blinking stupid. Nor would Polly, anymore. What's more, if Major Monroe is dead, that will make us all the more sure of it."

The telephone rang just then, startling them both out of their wits. Sadie held her breath as she watched Violet pick up the receiver and hold it to her ear.

The housekeeper kept murmuring, "I see, yes, I see," until Sadie could have screamed with frustration.

Finally, Violet hung up the receiver, but then stood quietly for long moments with her back still turned.

Staring at that rigid spine, Sadie felt sick. Afraid to ask, she could only wait, the feeling of dread growing ever stronger.

Elizabeth watched the sister hurry toward her, her fingers curled tightly in her palms.

Duane rose to his feet, his gaze also intent on the nurse as she reached them. She gave him a quick glance, then turned to Elizabeth.

"You may go in to see him," she said, her voice grave, "but I must ask you to stay only for a moment or two. I'm sorry to say the major's condition is extremely serious, and he must not be disturbed."

Elizabeth swallowed. She'd never been so frightened in all her life. If only her father were here to give her strength. He had always been there for her when she was growing up, a bastion of understanding, advice, and encouragement. But her father was gone . . . lost in the rubble of a bombed-out building, along with her dear departed mother. She'd lost so much, and now, it seemed, she was about to lose everything that remained to make her happy.

Her legs felt weak as she followed the sister down the long, narrow, bleak corridor, and she urged herself to remain strong. Pausing at the door to the ward, the sister turned to her. "Remember, no more than a minute or two."

Elizabeth nodded, then walked slowly into the quiet ward, braced for whatever might be facing her.

On either side, men lay silent in their beds, some with eyes closed, others staring at the ceiling, and some with their faces covered in bandages. As she passed each bed, her dread grew. She knew nothing about Earl's injuries, knew nothing about what to expect.

When she finally spotted him, her first reaction was a rush of relief. He wore no bandages around his head, and apart from a nasty graze across his pale cheek, his face was unmarked. In fact, if it hadn't been for his lack of color, she might have thought he was sleeping, so peaceful did he look with his dark head on the pillow, his strong features relaxed.

Upon further inspection, however, she noticed the bandages wrapped around his right arm, and a cage under the blankets suggested he had injuries to his legs. For a moment his pain was her pain, and she ached to hold him.

A chair had been placed by the side of the bed, and she sat down on it, hardly daring to breathe. She longed to call his name, touch his hand, anything to reassure herself that he was alive and knew she was there.

Instead she concentrated on the rise and fall of his chest beneath the white sheet, and prayed as she'd never prayed before. Mindful of the sister's warning, she sat for as long as she dared, then rose to go.

"I won't say good-bye," she whispered. "I'll just say get well, and I'll be back soon." She leaned over him and dropped a soft kiss on his forehead. He was so still, so unresponsive. Frightened, she stared at his chest again, relieved to see the steady rise and fall had not abated.

"Get well for me, my love," she whispered. "I need you so." Turning, she hurried out of the ward before she made a fool of herself and let the tears fall.

Duane Crawford stood as she hurried into the waiting room, his expression apprehensive.

Unable to speak just then, she simply shook her head.

"Come on," Duane said, taking hold of her arm, "I'll get you home."

She followed him out into the night, numb with weariness and a cold dread that would not subside, no matter how much she tried to look on the positive side.

He was a strong man, she tried to assure herself. Healthy, vigorous, and strong willed. He had survived what should have been a fatal crash, according to what she'd been told. He would come out of that hospital alive. She had to believe that or she'd go out of her mind.

Duane did his best to cheer her up on the long drive back to Sitting Marsh. His determinedly cheerful patter helped keep her mind from dwelling on the worst scenarios, and he even made her smile as they reached the long driveway up to the manor.

"I'm terribly grateful to you for giving up your time like this," she said as she climbed out of the jeep. "It was extremely kind of you to take me to the hospital, and I know how much your thoughtfulness would mean to Earl. Thank you so very much."

Duane touched his cap with the tips of his fingers. "My pleasure, ma'am. I just wish I'd had a car instead of having to take you in a jeep. It's not exactly a comfortable ride."

Elizabeth smiled. "It got me there, and that's all I could ask."

"Well, I reckon it's better than a horse and cart at that." He touched his cap again. "Good night, your ladyship."

Deep in thought, Elizabeth made her way between the hothouses around the mansion to the kitchen door. She found Violet had left the door unlocked, much to her relief. Opening it, Elizabeth was startled to see both Violet and Sadie seated at the kitchen table.

"Why aren't you in bed?" she demanded as they both turned to look at her.

"We were waiting for you to come home," Violet

said, staring at her with an odd expression on her face.

"How's the major, m'm?" Sadie asked anxiously.

"He's alive." Elizabeth slipped out of her coat and sank onto the empty chair. "That's all I really know right now."

"They wouldn't let you see him?" Violet asked.

"I saw him." Elizabeth let out her breath on a long sigh. "He was sedated. He didn't know I was there."

Sadie made a sympathetic tutting sound. "Was he banged up a lot?"

"Sadie!" Violet wagged a finger in her face. "You know better than to ask questions like that."

"I only wanted to know—," Sadie began, but Elizabeth interrupted.

"It's all right, Violet. I really don't know, Sadie. All I know is that his face seems to be unharmed."

"Well, that's good," Sadie said earnestly. "At least it weren't like Polly's Sam, with his face all messed up—"

"Sadie Buttons!" Once more Violet's harsh voice cut across the table. "I think it's time you went to bed."

Sadie sighed and pushed herself to her feet. "All right, I'm going. But don't forget to tell her ladyship the news."

Elizabeth looked at Violet. "What news?"

"It's Martin," Sadie began. "I thought someone was ringing to tell us something really terrible had happened to the major, but it wasn't that, it was—"

Again Violet cut her off. "Good *night*, Sadie."

Sadie shook her head, muttered a good-night, and disappeared out the door.

"What's all this about Martin?" Elizabeth felt another chill of fear. "He's all right, isn't he?"

"Oh, he's all, all right." Violet clicked her tongue. "I

mean, yes, he's not hurt or missing or anything. Though how in the world he got into this big a mess I'll never know."

Elizabeth laid her handbag on the empty chair next to Violet and buried her face in her hands. "Perhaps this had better wait until the morning. I really don't think I can take much more tonight."

"It's up to you," Violet said crisply, "but knowing you, you'll spend the night worrying and wondering about it, so you might as well hear it now. Besides, I'm not sure what it's all about anyway."

Elizabeth lowered her hands. "Violet, what on earth are you talking about?"

Violet sat back and folded her hands across her thin chest. "Martin has gone and got himself mixed up with the War Office, that's what."

"The War Office?"

"That's what I said. They rang here for him. Said to tell him to ring them in the morning." Violet shook her head. "How in the world did he get into trouble with the War Office?"

"I suppose we'll have to wait until the morning to ask him." Elizabeth looked hopefully at her housekeeper. "I don't suppose there's any tea in the pot?"

"If there is, it's cold by now." Violet peered more closely at her. "Besides, you look as if a stiff brandy would do you more good. I'll get you one."

She got up and crossed the kitchen to the dresser. "We've still got half a bottle left of the brandy the major brought us from the base." She poured some into a glass and brought it back to Elizabeth. "How is the major really, Lizzie? Is he going to be all right?"

Elizabeth took the glass and sipped some of the

brandy before setting it down. It burned hot fire in her chest, then settled in her stomach with a satisfying warmth that made her feel a little less bleak. "I honestly don't know, Violet. I wish I did. He looked so peaceful, as if he were simply asleep. I kept expecting him to wake up and . . ." She swallowed. "We'll know more in the morning, I expect."

Violet nodded. "I can't tell you how worried I was about you going all the way up there on that motorcycle. I don't know what your father would have said."

"I didn't take the motorcycle. That nice Captain Crawford took me in the jeep, along with most of the officers that are billeted here."

"Oh, that was nice of him." Violet went back to the dresser, poured herself a small brandy, and carried it back to the table. "If I'd known that I wouldn't have worried so."

"I suppose I should have let you know, but I was in such a hurry to get there—"

"It's all right, Lizzie. I know how upset you were."

"If it hadn't been for Captain Crawford, I don't know if I would have made it home tonight. He was kind enough to drive me back, even though the rest of his friends were off enjoying themselves in the town."

"Well, they won't be too long behind him," Violet said, glancing at the clock. "The pubs closed up well over an hour ago."

"Is it that late? I hadn't realized." Elizabeth picked up her glass. "I'm terribly sorry, Violet, for keeping you up like this."

Violet shook her head, then lifted her glass and drained it. She choked, cleared her throat, then said hoarsely, "I'm just glad you had someone drive you home. I don't know what I would have done if you'd stayed there all night."

"I would have rung to let you know." Elizabeth rubbed a weary hand across her eyes. "The captain sat with me for quite a while waiting to see if I could go in to see Earl. He told me about the town where he lives in Texas. It's not much bigger than Sitting Marsh apparently. He told me about the parades on July Fourth, and the horse and cart he rode in—"

She broke off, aware of the tingling feeling that nagged her to examine the comment she'd just made. There was a connection somewhere to the elusive piece of information that hovered on the edge of her memory.

"I think the horse-drawn carts are dying out," Violet murmured. "They're all changing over to motorcars and lorries nowadays. Can't remember when I last saw a horse and cart in the High Street—"

Elizabeth uttered a sharp exclamation.

Violet stared at her in concern. "You all right, Lizzie? You look so pale. You should go to bed."

Elizabeth finished her brandy and got up. "You're right, I should. I have a lot to take care of tomorrow." She gathered up her handbag and threw her coat over her arm. "You go to bed as well, Violet. You need your sleep." She turned and hurried out of the kitchen, leaving Violet to stare after her.

Of course. She could see it quite clearly now. The coast road, bathed in moonlight, she and Violet standing by the motorcycle, screaming Martin's name and hearing nothing except the wind in the trees . . . *and the sound of a horse's hooves.*

She hadn't thought much about it at the time. It was a common enough sound in the countryside, and she and

Violet had been worried about finding Martin. Apparently it never occurred to either of them to wonder why a horse would be trotting along the country lanes in the dark so late at night.

Most of the horse-drawn carts in the area belonged to the farmers, and they would be fast asleep, since they would rise before the dawn. There was, however, someone else who had a horse and cart. Clyde Morgan.

It was, indeed, very late for him to be out collecting his rags and bones. Then again, that was the night Morgan had died, and his midnight ride might very well have been his last. If he had died in his own front room, as she suspected, then someone would have had to take him to the ruined factory. A horse and cart would have made a most convenient conveyance for a dead body.

Tomorrow, right after ringing the hospital, she would take a look at Clyde Morgan's cart. If she found what she suspected she would find, then her suspicions would be confirmed. Then she would once again be faced with the inevitable question. What on earth was she going to do about it?

CHAPTER
✿16✿

Despite the turmoil churning in her mind, exhaustion took over and Elizabeth slept soundly that night. She awoke with a start, memory flooding back to jolt her fully awake and propel her out of bed.

The closest telephone was in her office, and she threw on a dressing gown, tying the sash as she sped along the corridor.

Once inside her office, she grabbed up the receiver, her trembling fingers dialing the number she had scribbled on her blotting pad.

A brisk female voice answered her, and for a moment she froze, unable to ask the question for fear of the answer. The woman on the end of the line sounded impatient as she repeated her greeting, and Elizabeth took a deep breath.

"Good morning," she said breathlessly. "I'm Lady Elizabeth, from the Manor House in Sitting Marsh. I'm inquiring as to the condition of Major Earl Monroe."

The silence on the end of the line terrified her, but then the voice spoke again. "Your ladyship, the major had a reasonably comfortable night and is resting."

Elizabeth closed her eyes. He'd survived the night. Thank God. "Is he any better?"

"You'd have to ask the doctor about that, m'm. He's not available at this moment."

"Very well." Elizabeth glanced at the clock. "When can I speak to the doctor?"

"He's doing his rounds, m'm. He should be done in an hour or two, if you'd care to try again later."

"I intend to visit the major later today. I can speak to the doctor then." She hung up before the woman could tell her no visitors were allowed. No one was going to prevent her from seeing Earl today. No one.

After getting dressed, she hurried down to the kitchen. As usual, Violet was at her post at the stove, and both Polly and Sadie were seated at the table.

"I forgot to tell you last night, m'm, but we caught the knickers thief," Sadie announced, apparently unaffected by Violet's disapproving click of the tongue.

"You mean thieves," Polly added.

Elizabeth ate her porridge and listened as the two girls filled her in on their adventures of the day before. "How in heaven's name are you going to return all that underwear?" she asked when they had finished. "How will you know what belongs to whom?"

"We thought about that, m'm," Sadie said, throwing a triumphant grin in Polly's direction. "We're going to put them all out on a table in Polly's front garden, and then let everyone know they can come by and pick out what belongs to them."

"Yeah," Polly chimed in. "Violet's already picked

out yours and hers, and Sadie and me have got ours, so the rest belong to whoever had them stolen."

"I," Violet interrupted, with a frown at Polly. "Sadie and *I*."

"Well, I've got mine, too," Polly muttered, looking confused.

"We did think about taking them down to the police station, m'm," Sadie said, "but can you imagine George or Sid trying to sort that lot out?"

Polly giggled, and Violet's frown deepened. "Well, all I can say," she said crisply, "is that it's a very good job it was only young boys in that windmill. If it had been some dangerous criminal, you and Polly would have been in quite a pickle."

"Not really," Polly said, nudging Sadie with her elbow. "We had the whole American army out there."

"Army air force," Sadie corrected. "Joe's always telling me as how he's in the air force but it's attached to the army, so it's army air force. That's why they call it the USAAF."

Elizabeth frowned. "What were the Americans doing there anyway?"

Sadie shrugged. "Didn't have time to ask them. They got rid of us in a hurry."

"Per'aps they were looking for the thief, too," Polly suggested.

"I'm sure they've got better things to do than hunt down a pack of delinquents who go around stealing washing from a line," Violet muttered.

"Which makes one wonder exactly what the American army was doing there." Elizabeth turned to Sadie. "Didn't they give you any idea why they were there?"

"Nope." Sadie thought about it. "They had their guns

drawn, though, so I think they were expecting more than what they got."

Elizabeth glanced at the clock. "Well, I can't worry about that now. I have an errand to run, then I'm going into North Horsham." She looked at Polly. "I trust you'll be able to take care of things today?"

Polly nodded and jumped up from the table. "Of course, m'm. Don't you worry about a thing. I'll take care of everything. I'll be off now and get started."

"You'd better get started, too, young lady." Violet pointed a bony finger at Sadie. "There's plenty to be done now that the boys in the east wing are back."

"Don't I know it." Sadie got to her feet. "I hope you find the major in better health, m'm," she said, earning herself a grateful smile from Elizabeth.

The door had barely closed behind the girls when it opened again and Martin shuffled in.

Elizabeth was concerned to see the dark shadows under his eyes. She waited for what seemed an eternity for him to cross the short space between the door and his chair. He finally came to an unsteady halt and blinked at her over the rims of his spectacles.

"Good morning, madam. May I be permitted to join you at the table?"

"Of course you may, Martin."

"Thank you, madam. I am much obliged."

She made herself stay seated while he struggled to lower himself on the chair, knowing if she didn't he would refuse to sit. She needed to have a word with him, and the less time spent doing so the better.

Finally settling himself, Martin looked at Violet. "So what poisonous concoction have you whipped up for the feast this morning? Not more of that loathsome porridge, I trust."

Violet sniffed and turned back to the stove. "You could always go and eat corn with the chickens."

A puzzled frown marred Martin's brow. "I wasn't aware we kept chickens on the estate."

"We don't," Violet snapped. "I was talking about Farmer Miller's chickens."

This was apparently too much for Martin to comprehend.

While he was still working on it, Elizabeth leaned forward. "The telephone rang for you last night."

An odd expression flickered across his face. "I didn't hear it."

Violet tutted. "Because you were in bed, you silly old goat."

Martin sent her a withering glance. "Well, that would certainly explain why, of course."

"It was the War Office," Elizabeth watched his face closely, but couldn't be sure if he'd understood.

"The War Office, madam?"

"Yes, Martin. They asked that you give them a ring this morning."

"Very well, madam."

Elizabeth waited, while Violet turned to face them, sticky porridge clinging to the wooden spoon in her hand.

When it became apparent that Martin had nothing more to say, Elizabeth tried again. "Martin, why would the War Office want you to ring them?"

"Why don't you ask them, madam?"

"I'm asking you, Martin." She wasn't in the least comfortable with the situation. On the one hand, it was really none of her business. On the other hand, since she was responsible for Martin's welfare, she had to make it her business. If Martin was in trouble, he would need her help.

Martin stared at his empty plate for a long time, then said in a matter-of-fact voice, "I rather imagine it's a military secret and therefore I'm unable to discuss it."

"Is it also a military secret that a very posh motorcar brought you home late last night?" Violet demanded.

Elizabeth looked at her in surprise. "You didn't tell me that last night."

"I forgot about it, didn't I." Violet looked at Martin. "Well? What about this motorcar then? What was that all about?"

Martin gave her a blank look. "Motorcar?"

"Sadie saw you, so don't pretend with me." Violet crossed her thin arms over her chest. "You'd better tell us what this is all about, Martin Chezzlewit, before they throw you in prison."

"Really, Martin," Elizabeth added. "You have both of us quite worried. I do think you should tell us what this is all about."

Martin started fidgeting with the handle of his teacup. "All I'm at liberty to say, madam, is that I have been helping the War Office in a delicate matter."

Elizabeth stared at him in astonishment, until the long silence was broken by a guffaw of laughter from Violet.

"Hark at him," she spluttered. "He thinks he's a blinking secret service agent."

Only Elizabeth glimpsed the gleam in Martin's eyes, then it was gone. "You might say that," he murmured.

Giving up, Elizabeth rose. "Well, I'd better be off."

Martin struggled to get to his feet again, but Elizabeth was already at the door.

"I don't know what time I'll be back from the hospital," she said, "so don't expect me for meals. I'll try to ring you later to let you know what I'm doing."

"That would be nice," Violet said dryly.

Elizabeth let the door close behind her, still wondering what was behind the mystery with Martin. It was obvious something was going on, but she knew her butler well enough to know that if he didn't want to tell her anything there was nothing she could do to persuade him. Eventually it would all come out, no doubt, when he was ready for her to know. Since no harm had befallen him thus far, she just had to trust that happy state of affairs would continue.

Once outside the house, however, her thoughts turned to the matter at hand. She had no idea where Clyde Morgan kept his horse and cart, but she had to assume it was somewhere close by.

The obvious place would be one of the farms, where they often rented out a stable. There were three close enough to be convenient for Clyde Morgan, and she rode down to the one nearest his house. Her search proved fruitless. None of the farmers she visited admitted to stabling Clyde Morgan's horse and cart.

The morning was almost over as she made her way back to town. Rather than go back to the manor, she stopped in at Bessie's bake shop with the intention of snatching a quick bite before going on to North Horsham.

Bessie was delighted to see her, and insisted on joining her at her table for a few minutes, despite the crowded tearoom which kept her waitresses hopping.

"You'll never guess what Rita Crumm's lot have been up to now," she said as Elizabeth bit into a piece of tasty Cornish pasty. "They had George call the American base and tell them there were an army of Germans hiding in the old windmill. The Yanks went charging out there and all it were was a bunch of schoolboys playing tricks." Bessie's hearty laughter turned heads in the quiet room. "Talk about looking daft. I bet they don't show their faces in town for a while."

"Ah, so that's why the Americans were out there." Elizabeth dabbed her mouth with her serviette. "I wondered what they were doing at the windmill."

"Oh, so you heard about it, then?"

Bessie looked disappointed, until Elizabeth explained the whole story, then she chuckled.

"I tell you, never a dull moment in Sitting Marsh, that's for sure."

Elizabeth picked up her knife and fork again. "We certainly have our share of unusual situations. Speaking of which, I don't suppose you know where the rag and bone man kept his horse and cart, by any chance?"

Bessie grinned. "I always say, your ladyship, that if you want to know something, you come to Bessie's tea shop. Hear everything, we do here, and if one of us don't know, t'other does."

"Then you do know where he kept them?"

Bessie put her finger alongside her nose. "Well, I did hear as how he kept them in a shed in the field behind his house. Along with all the castoffs he collected. I'd like to take a look in there meself. I reckon that shed is full of good rubbish."

"I'm sure it is," Elizabeth murmured, remembering the crowded walls in Iris's house. She glanced at the clock over the huge brick fireplace. "I'll take the bill now, Bessie. I'm in rather a hurry."

"Right you are, your ladyship." Bessie heaved her plump body out of the chair. "Be right back with it, I will."

Elizabeth swallowed the rest of her pasty, took a few sips of her tea, then gathered up her handbag. She would just have time to stop by the Morgans' house before setting off for North Horsham and the hospital.

A few minutes later she arrived at the end of the lane and parked her motorcycle out of sight from the house. An alleyway ran down between the houses, leading onto the fields behind them. Hurrying as fast as she could, Elizabeth headed down the path.

She spotted the shed as soon as she emerged from the alleyway, and after a furtive glance around to make sure no one was in the back gardens, she crossed the field to the ramshackle building.

As she opened the door it creaked loudly, and a soft whinny answered her. The horse stood in the corner, its head lifted in expectation, its ears flattened against its head. It looked dejected and underfed. Elizabeth made a mental note to send a member of the S.P.C.A. around to take a look at it later.

She spoke to it softly as she squeezed past piles of boxes to where the cart stood. A pale shaft of light struggled to penetrate the grimy window, but it was enough to see inside the cart. It didn't take much scrutiny to find what she was looking for. A large dark stain on the floor of the cart told the story.

It was as she suspected. Afraid that her husband would harm her children, Iris Morgan had shot him and carried his body in the cart to the damaged munitions factory, knowing it was to be bulldozed down the next morning. No doubt she hoped the body would never be found, but just in case, she had put the gun in her dead husband's hand to make it look like suicide.

Elizabeth turned back to the door. She knew now what she had to do. She could not, in all good conscience, allow this crime to go unpunished. Not even for the sake of the children. Clyde Morgan might well have been a monster, but it was not up to his wife to take the law into her own hands. Iris Morgan had to answer for what she had done, and it would be up to the courts to decide a fitting punishment.

Having come to that decision, Elizabeth felt a small measure of relief. The quandary had worried her a good deal, and right now she had far too much to worry about as it was. She would go immediately to George, tell him what she knew, and insist he inform the inspector right away.

She had her hand outstretched to open the door when to her dismay it was shoved open, bruising her fingers. Iris stood in the doorway, a wicked-looking carving knife in her hand. "It's too bad you didn't mind your own business, Lady Elizabeth," she said, brandishing the knife in Elizabeth's face. "Now I'm afraid I'll have to shut you up for good."

Cold with shock, Elizabeth fell back. "This is ridiculous," she said, striving to put authority in her voice. "You can't just go around killing people and hope to get away with it."

"I got away with Clyde's, didn't I?" Iris advanced into the shed. "I'll get away with yours, too."

"You didn't exactly get away with your husband's murder," Elizabeth said, frantically playing for time.

"After all, I worked out what happened. Other people will, too, eventually." Out of the corner of her eye, she saw the horse shift back and forth. If she could work her way closer to it, she might be able to create enough commotion to escape. She began edging toward the corner where the horse stood, ears twitching, watching the scene in front of him.

"I made mistakes with Clyde," Iris said, her calm voice all the more horrifying. "I didn't have time to work things out. But I've been thinking a lot about what to do about you if you got too nosy." She shot a glance over her shoulder, then raised her voice. "Tommy! You can come in now."

Elizabeth's hopes faded as the boy appeared in the doorway. He carried a length of rope in his hands, and looked every bit as determined as his mother.

"I've got it all worked out," Iris said, beckoning to her son. "We tie you up in here and wait until it gets dark. Then we take you and your motorcycle to the top of the cliffs and then over you go. The tide will be in, so if the fall doesn't kill you, you'll drown in the sea. Too bad, Lady Elizabeth. You drove your motorcycle up the coast road and missed the curve in the dark. Such a shame. Now there'll be no more lady of the manor in Sitting Marsh."

She signaled to Tommy once more and he came forward, his face a stiff mask.

Elizabeth stared at him in horror. She couldn't die now. Not when so many people needed her. Earl, lying helpless in a hospital bed. Martin, up to heaven knew what with the War Office. Violet, Polly, Sadie . . . her tenants in the village . . . What would they all do without her?

She saw Earl's white, motionless face lying on the pillow, his still body beneath the covers. This was not the last image she wanted of him. She wanted to see him well and happy before they parted forever.

Heedless of the knife in Iris's hands, Elizabeth plunged toward the boy. Raising an arm, she swept him out of the way, hitting him hard in the shoulder so that he stumbled. She was almost at the door when something exploded in her head. Lights flashed, the world spun, and then everything faded into silent darkness.

CHAPTER

❧ 17 ❧

It was late afternoon before Martin finally used the telephone to ring the War Office. Violet knew that because she'd followed him around all day, waiting unashamedly to eavesdrop on the conversation.

She'd deliberately stayed out of the kitchen, once it became obvious that Martin had no intention of using the telephone while she was within earshot. After lunch, while Martin was still in the kitchen, she'd made a point of telling Sadie that she was going to the market that afternoon, and had even put on her felt hat and gloves and fetched the shopping bags from the pantry.

She hadn't been gone more than ten minutes, hovering outside the back door, when she heard Martin lift the telephone from its hook. Since he was ringing all the way to London, she knew it would take a while for everything to connect, which gave her plenty of time to run around to the east wing steps, enter the great hall, and run the length of it to reach Elizabeth's office.

Once there, she had to wait a moment or two to catch her breath. Martin was bound to hear all that huffing and puffing if she didn't. She considered it her duty to find out what was going on. After all, there were people out there who took advantage of elderly gentlemen like Martin, and someone had to look out for the old fool. Lizzie would thank her for taking care of matters.

Having thus satisfied her conscience, Violet felt no qualms about lifting the telephone in Lizzie's office to listen in.

After carefully lifting the receiver from its hook, she held her breath and pressed the telephone to her ear. She was just in time to hear Martin's quavery voice telling someone his name.

Violet listened to the entire conversation, then waited for Martin to hang up the telephone downstairs before replacing the receiver.

She was at the door when the telephone jangled, scaring her half out of her wits. She waited through a couple of the double rings, then picked up the receiver again. Martin must have gone back to his room. Not that he ever answered the telephone. Always complained he couldn't hear a word through that newfangled trumpet. Which didn't stop him from using it when it was convenient for him, of course.

Holding the receiver to her ear, she said warily, "The Manor House. This is the housekeeper speaking."

A woman's voice answered her. "This is Sister Brown at North Horsham General Hospital. I wish to speak to Lady Elizabeth, if you please."

Violet peered at the clock on Lizzie's desk. It was almost five o'clock. "Her ladyship is not present," she said, a faint worry beginning to niggle at her. "In fact, I was under the impression she was at the hospital."

"Ah, well, that's what I wanted to speak to her about. She inquired about the health of Major Monroe, and I wanted to tell her that the doctor has given his permission for the major to receive visitors. Major Monroe is awake and wishes to see her."

Violet frowned. "But she should be there by now. In fact, I was expecting her to come home again soon. Are you sure she's not visiting the major?"

"I just looked in on him ten minutes ago," the sister assured her, "and he hasn't had any visitors at all today."

"Well, as soon as I see her ladyship I'll be sure to pass on the message." Violet paused, then added, "Perhaps you'll ask her to give me a ring if she should arrive there?"

"Certainly."

"Please give my best to the major." Violet put down the telephone, the worry beginning to grow. Where on earth could Lizzie be if she wasn't at the hospital? She tried to remember exactly what Elizabeth had said that morning. *I have an errand to run, then I'm going into North Horsham.* What kind of errand would keep her busy all day, especially when she was so anxious to see the major? It didn't make sense.

Her stomach knotted with worry now, Violet hurried back to the kitchen. If only Lizzie had told her what errand she was going to run, she might have been able to track her down.

She lifted the telephone and started dialing George's number, then hung up again. There was no point in raising an alarm if it wasn't necessary. It wasn't as if

Lizzie were chasing after a murderer or anything, like she sometimes did.

Violet turned away from the telephone, then changed her mind again. Lizzie must have eaten somewhere that day, and Bessie's tea shop seemed the likely place.

Bessie answered her ring, sounding rushed and out of breath.

"I was wondering if her ladyship dropped by today," Violet said, doing her best to sound unconcerned.

"Yes," Bessie said, her voice tinged with impatience. "She was here. Had a Cornish pasty and left."

"What time was that?"

"Around one o'clock, I suppose. I know we were busy. Just like we are now."

Ignoring the hint, Violet demanded, "Did she say where she was going after that?"

There was a pause while Bessie answered someone in the background, then she spoke into the telephone again. "No, she didn't." She seemed about to hang up, then added, "Is something wrong?"

"No, no," Violet hastily assured her. "I was just wondering if she was coming home for supper, that's all."

"She didn't say. She did ask about Clyde Morgan's horse, now I come to think about it. She might have called in there."

Violet thanked her and hung up. Her face creased in a frown, she sat down at the kitchen table. Why on earth would Lizzie be asking about the rag and bone man's horse? Clyde Morgan was dead. Was she thinking about buying his horse? Surely not. She had enough trouble taking care of the two hounds the major had given her.

Violet's frown deepened. In a million years she would never have thought that Lizzie would spend all day seeing about a horse when her major was waiting for her in a hospital bed in North Horsham. Something was wrong. She could feel it in her bones. Maybe it wouldn't hurt to ring George after all.

Elizabeth slowly opened her eyes and blinked. Searing pain stabbed through her head when she turned it, and she uttered a soft moan. She lay on her side, and the arm pinned beneath her had gone to sleep. She tried moving it, but her hands seemed to be tied together. She couldn't open her mouth. Something soft had been tied over it.

The air was unbearably stuffy, and an awful smell invaded her nostrils. Hearing a soft shuffling sound, she braved the pain to lift her head. She appeared to be in a shed, with a horse for company.

In the next instant it all came flooding back. Iris Morgan had attacked her, ordered her son to tie her up, and intended to throw her and her motorcycle over the cliff to make it look like an accident.

Groaning in pain, Elizabeth eased herself over onto her back and stared at the beams above her head. No one knew she was there. Violet thought she was in North Horsham visiting Earl. There was no hope of escape. She couldn't even call out.

Just to make sure, she drew in a deep breath through her nose and tried to force it out in a shout. All she got for her efforts was a muffled whine and another vicious stab of pain in her head.

Moving her bound feet, she winced when her ankle came in contact with something sharp. With great caution she angled her head, and realized she was lying in the cart, alongside her motorcycle.

She lay back, her spirits plummeting. Was this how it was all going to end? Would Earl survive, only to find out she had died in a so-called accident after driving over a cliff? What would that do to his recovery?

No! She could not, would not, let it happen. She turned her head again and examined the motorcycle. Her ankle had collided with the edge of the mudguard. Was it sharp enough to cut through the rope that bound her hands? It was worth a try.

The pain in her head almost blinded her as she wriggled around to get her hands in position. At long last she was there, and she pressed the rope against the mudguard and began sawing.

She sawed until her arms felt as if they would drop off from fatigue, but the thought of Earl lying in that hospital bed kept her at it. Just when she thought she could not move her arms one more inch, she felt the rope begin to give.

Her determination renewed, she sawed even more frantically. So intent was she on breaking through the final strands, she didn't hear the shed door open. It wasn't until she heard his voice that she realized Tommy had come back into the shed and stood not five feet away from her.

Tears of frustration coursed down her cheeks as she stared into eyes that were empty of expression. Her muffled protest, unintelligible behind the cloth over her mouth, went unheeded. He stepped toward her, the carving knife in his hand, and she closed her eyes. *Goodbye, my love. I'm so sorry.*

She bit back her whimper of fear as rough hands turned her on her side. She waited for the knife to sink in her back, wondering why Iris had sent this young boy to commit this terrible deed.

Then her body jerked in surprise when her hands were suddenly freed. Before she could fully comprehend what was happening, her feet were also cut free. The cloth was removed from her mouth, with a silent signal from the boy to stay quiet.

He needn't have worried. Her soaring hope had rendered her speechless.

Stunned by this turn of events, she allowed him to help her from the cart. Blood rushed back into her cramped limbs, and she bit back a cry of pain, fearful that it might cause him to turn on her with the knife he still held in his hand.

"Come on," he whispered, and led her stumbling and limping to the door.

With an unbelievable heady rush of relief, she stepped outside into the cool evening air.

"Go," the boy whispered urgently. "Run, before she comes to get you."

Her resolve fast returning, Elizabeth took the boy's arm. "I can't leave you here with her. She's insane. She killed your father—"

The boy shook his head, cutting off her words. "Mum didn't kill our dad." He swallowed, and sent a scared look at the house. "I did it. He beat me and then he was going to beat Katie again. I couldn't let him do that. I was afraid he'd kill her. I got the gun and I was just going to frighten him with it. I didn't know there was a bullet in it." Tears rolled down the boy's face, and his voice trembled on a sob. "I had to stop him from hurting Katie, didn't I."

"Of course you did," Elizabeth said soothingly. "I understand. But now we have to tell—"

"Tomm-y-y-y-y!" Iris's voice floated down the alley-way.

Tommy shoved Elizabeth away with both hands. "Go! She'll kill you. She said she wouldn't let anyone take me away. She means it. I couldn't let her do that because of what I did. I just couldn't."

"I'm not leaving you with her." Elizabeth turned to face the alleyway as Iris's voice sounded louder. "We'll face her together and we'll get Katie and—"

"No!" Tommy was sobbing now—huge, deep sobs that tore at her heart. "You can't take Katie away, you can't!"

"Tommy—" There was no time to argue with the boy. Elizabeth grabbed the knife out of his hand and turned to face the woman running toward them.

Just then another shout echoed across the quiet field. Someone hurtled out of the alleyway on a bicycle. Some-one short and stout—George. Somehow he wedged his bicycle in front of Iris, stopping her cold.

For a moment it seemed as if she would fight him, but then she burst into tears and sank to the ground. Tommy broke free from Elizabeth's grip and ran toward his mother. Dropping to his knees beside her, he wound his arms around her, his sobs joining hers.

"Thank goodness I thought to call Bessie," Violet said, some time later. She set a glass of brandy down on the kitchen table in front of Elizabeth. "If she hadn't said that about you talking about Clyde Morgan's horse, I never would have thought of calling George until much later, and by then it might have been too late."

She shivered and poured herself a generous glass from the brandy bottle. "I tell you, when George rang to tell me you'd almost been killed, I was beside myself." She glared at Elizabeth. "Why didn't you tell me that the rag and bone man was murdered and you were getting yourself involved again?"

Elizabeth took down a mouthful of brandy and shuddered. "I didn't know for certain and since George was so convinced it was suicide I didn't want to make any accusations until I was sure that my suspicions were founded."

Violet seemed about ready to cry. "You always confide in me, Lizzie. I don't know why you didn't this time."

"You were so worried about Martin. I didn't want to worry you with something else that might well have been nothing more than my imagination."

Violet wagged a finger at her. "Don't you ever do that to me again, Elizabeth. From now on you tell me when you're going off on one of your wild-goose chases. If no one knows where you are, how do we know when you're in trouble? It was lucky the hospital rang or I'd—"

Elizabeth sat up straight in her chair. "The hospital? What did they say? Did they say anything about Earl?"

"Of course they said something about the major," Violet said crossly. "Why else would they call?"

"What did they say?" Elizabeth took hold of Violet's hands. "Violet, tell me, what did they say?"

"They said as how the major was awake and wanted to see you, but—"

Elizabeth waited to hear no more. She leapt to her feet, sending her empty glass spinning across the table. "I must go to him."

"What now?" Violet deftly caught the glass and set it upright. "It's past eight o'clock. You'll never get there before dark. Besides, the major's probably asleep by now."

Elizabeth stared at the clock. "I had no idea it was that late." She rushed over to the telephone and grabbed it off the hook. "I'll ring the hospital and ask how he is." Her fingers busily dialed as she spoke.

Violet said something she didn't hear, but she paid scant attention. All her thoughts were on Earl now, and as she waited for someone to answer the urgent ringing of the phone, she prayed she would hear good news.

It took some time before she could persuade the nurse who answered to allow her to speak to someone in charge. When the sister finally came onto the phone, she was obviously annoyed.

"I must advise you, your ladyship," she said stiffly, "that it's past visiting hours. I must ask you to ring us back in the morning."

"I just want to know the condition of Major Earl Monroe," Elizabeth said stubbornly.

"The nurse could have told you that."

"I didn't want a carefully worded stock answer. I need to know his real condition." Elizabeth waited a beat, then added, "Or should I just come in person to find out what I want to know?"

"The major is resting right now." The sister hesitated, then added, "He's over the crisis, and is expected to recover." Elizabeth's cry of joy made her pause, then she added, "I must warn you, however, it's likely to be a long process. It's better that you talk to the doctor in the morning. He can tell you more than I can."

Elizabeth hugged the telephone to her cheek. "Thank you, sister. I'll be there first thing."

She hung up the receiver and turned to find Violet dabbing away at the corner of her eye with her handkerchief. "He's going to be all right," she said and, in a burst of joy, hugged Violet's scrawny body. "He's going to be well!"

"Thank the good Lord." Violet patted Elizabeth's hand. "Now sit down. I have something to tell you about Martin."

Elizabeth sat. No matter what trouble Martin was in, they could take care of it. Now that Earl was on the mend, she could take care of anything.

"I think Martin has gone completely off his rocker," Violet said.

Except that, Elizabeth thought. "Now what?"

Violet nodded. "I heard him talking to someone on the telephone. I think someone is pretending to be from the War Office and they're humoring him. I wouldn't be surprised if two men in white coats turn up at the door one morning to take him away."

"Why? What did he say?"

"Not much. He just said his name, and the gentleman on the other end told him he'd done an excellent job and his country was grateful to him."

"Oh, my goodness." Elizabeth ran a hand over her hair and winced as her fingers came in contact with a large bump on her head.

"Let me look at that." Violet jumped up and began parting Elizabeth's hair.

"I do know Martin was involved with the government in some way in the first world war. Something to do with breaking codes, I believe. Apparently Martin taught the Morse code to sailors at the turn of the century and was an expert at breaking codes. Ouch!"

Her yelp of pain stilled Violet's probing fingers. "I'll get a cold cloth for that." She hurried over to the sink and turned on the tap. "Well, that explains it, then. You know how Martin is, always getting confused. He must have thought it was World War One again and offered his services. The War Office must have got a good laugh out of that one. Can you imagine Martin trying to break a code nowadays? Half the time he doesn't know where he is or what he's doing."

"Well, it's nice of the War Office to humor him." Elizabeth shook her head, then wished she hadn't when pain sliced through it. "I must call them and thank them for being so understanding."

Violet held a cloth under the water, then squeezed it out. "Well, they certainly went to a lot of trouble, picking him up in that fancy motorcar and all. I asked him about that and he said it was a chariot and it took him to the stars."

Her hands stilled, and she stared at Elizabeth. "Funny about that motorcar. You don't suppose . . ."

They stared at each other for a long moment, then in unison shook their heads, muttering, "No, of course not. It couldn't be."

"That's what I thought," Violet said, sounding relieved. "Barmy, he is. Completely barmy."

And if it made them more comfortable to believe that, Elizabeth decided, then who was she to question it.

The night seemed endless, with Elizabeth tossing and turning, dozing fitfully until at last she could pull back the blackout curtains and allow the morning light to creep into the room.

An hour later she was on her way to North Horsham,

riding her motorcycle at a reckless pace that had her arriving at the hospital in record time. After a frustrating wait for the doctor to finish his rounds, she was finally allowed in to see Earl.

She found him propped up on his pillow, his face still drawn and pale, but his eyes now open. The covers were still tented over his legs, and now she noticed the thick bandages strapped around his upper body.

His eyes lit up when he saw her, and, mindful of the nurse hovering over him, not to mention the dozen or so other patients in the ward, she had to restrain her impulse to rush over to him and throw herself on the bed.

Instead, she had to make do with small talk while the nurse bustled about the room, drawing curtains, straightening bedclothes, tidying the bedside table, until Elizabeth wanted to scream at her to leave them alone.

At long last, the nurse drew the curtains around the bed to give them some privacy, reminded Elizabeth she had only a few minutes, and left.

"Come here," Earl said softly as the curtain swished closed behind the nurse. He held out his hand, and Elizabeth took it, concerned to find his fingers so cold.

"You had us all quite concerned," she told him as she bent over to drop a kiss on his cheek.

Taking her by surprise, he turned his head and her mouth landed on his. She kept it there for a few satisfying seconds before seating herself again.

"Sister told me you were here a couple of days ago." His gaze probed hers. "I guess I was asleep. I was kinda hoping you'd stop by yesterday."

"I intended to, but—" She paused, wondering how much to tell him.

"Something more important turned up, huh?"

"Of course not." She clasped his hand tighter in hers. "Nothing is more important to me than you. I thought you knew that."

He didn't answer her, but kept his gaze steadily on her face.

She sighed and looked down at their clasped hands. "I was . . . detained on my way to see you."

His eyes narrowed. "Elizabeth, just what aren't you telling me?"

In the end she told him all of it. From the beginning, when she first suspected Clyde Morgan had been murdered, to her visits to the three people she thought had motives for murder, to her narrow escape the day before.

As she talked, his expression gradually grew more serious, until he was actually scowling at her. "You promised me you would be careful."

"I really didn't expect Iris to attack me." She shuddered at the memory. "I just wanted to confirm my suspicions. I couldn't make up my mind what to do about it until I was sure. I had those children to think about. . . . I was afraid that Iris had become unbalanced and that the children were in danger."

"Why didn't you take George along with you?"

"I couldn't convince him it was murder and I needed proof."

"So you risked your life. If it hadn't been for that boy . . ." He shifted his body and grimaced in pain.

"I know, I know." She felt terrible causing him this much distress. She wanted to take care of him, take away the pain, make him forget his injuries and see him smile again.

"So what's going to happen to them all?"

"I talked to the inspector last night. He thinks the boy will have to go into a remand home for a while. Katie has an aunt who is willing to take her until the family can be together again. I'm afraid Iris will have to pay for her part in concealing what happened and for attacking me. I spoke on her behalf, however, and considering the circumstances, the inspector thinks the sentence won't be too harsh."

"That was real generous of you, considering she planned on murdering you."

"She was protecting her child," Elizabeth said. "I can understand how she must have felt. Anyway, let's not talk about all this now. It's over, and I'm safe and well. Now we have to concentrate on getting you well."

"I'm working on it." He gave her a stern look. "Once I'm out of this bed, you and I are going to have a long discussion about your meddling in murder."

She raised her eyebrows. "Meddling? I see it as my civic duty. My people need to be protected."

"And who's going to protect you?"

She lowered her gaze. "Well, we can discuss it once you're out of that bed."

"I can promise you one thing, your gorgeous ladyship. Once I'm out of this bed I'm not wasting time on discussion."

She looked up, relieved to see his faint grin. One thing she knew for certain. She had come so close to losing him this time. They'd been offered a second chance, and if only they were given a little more time together, she would no longer let protocol get in the way. Whoever said it was better to have loved and lost knew what he was talking about.

She loved Major Earl Monroe with all her heart and

if she was destined to have her heart broken, at least she would have known what it was to love him completely—physically and emotionally—and she could live on the memories for the rest of her life.

And to hell with protocol.

His gruff voice interrupted her thoughts. "What are you looking so serious about now?"

She tightened her grasp on his hand. "I was just thinking that we've wasted a lot of time worrying about things that don't really matter."

His gaze was intent on her face now, as if he were trying to read her mind. "Like what?"

She tried to pass it off with a shrug. "Oh, I don't know, really. Protocol, appearances, obligations to people, I suppose. Things like that."

He seemed to be having some difficulty responding to that. After a long pause he said quietly, "You do know that they'll be sending me back home when I get out of here?"

She could almost feel her heart breaking in half. "I thought you might be going home, yes." Until he'd actually spoken the words, she'd made herself believe it couldn't happen. Now there was no avoiding it. She prayed she wouldn't cry until she was out of his sight.

"There's something else I should tell you."

He let out a long sigh, and she gritted her teeth. She had to be brave. For his sake. If this was to be the last time she saw him after all, she wanted him to remember her smiling.

"I wanted to wait until I was out of this bed, so I could do things right, but what I need to say can't wait. It's better I say it now and get it over with."

Her throat felt so tight she was afraid she wouldn't

be able to breathe. He was trying to say good-bye. In spite of her best efforts, an embarrassing tear squeezed out of her eye and dribbled down her cheek.

"My divorce is final," Earl said, squeezing her hand so tightly it hurt. "I'm a free man."

She blinked, struggling to understand what he was trying to say.

He closed his eyes for a brief moment, then muttered, "Aw, hell. I love you, Elizabeth. Marry me. Come back with me to Wyoming, where we'll raise horses and live out the rest of our lives together."

She gulped, completely at a loss how to answer him. She'd dreamed of this moment, longed for it. Now it was here she was lost in confusion. How could she leave Sitting Marsh and the Manor House? "Polly and Sadie will manage without me. They're young and would have moved on in time anyway. But how can I leave Martin and Violet behind?"

She hadn't realized she'd spoken out loud until Earl said, "Bring them with you. I've always thought it would be nice to have servants."

"Domestics," she murmured, her mind still trying to grasp the wonderful, incredible offer he was making.

"You could turn the Manor House over to the government as a historical monument," Earl said. "I've been giving this a lot of thought lying here, and—"

With a muffled cry of joy she smothered his words with her mouth. His kiss was very satisfying, considering his weak condition. When she raised her head, the love in his eyes took her breath away. "I love you, too," she whispered.

He grinned. "It's about time you told me that. Does this mean you'll come home with me?"

"Yes." She sat back on her chair, her hand still clinging to his. "Yes, my love. I'll marry you and go with you anywhere you want to take me."

She thought she just might drown in his beautiful smile when he gave her a broad wink and murmured softly, "Atta girl."

TELL THE WORLD THIS BOOK WAS

GOOD	BAD	SO-SO

Lord Woolton Pie

1 pound each of diced potatoes, cauliflower,
    swedes [rutabaga], and carrots
3 or 4 green onions
1 teaspoon vegetable extract
1 tablespoon oatmeal
Chopped parsley

Boil all ingredients for ten minutes, using just enough water to cover. Stir occasionally to prevent sticking. Allow to cool, place in pie dish, and cover with crust of mashed potatoes or pastry. Bake in moderate oven (350°), until crust is brown, and serve hot with gravy.
Feeds five to six people.

A British government recipe.

KATE KINGSBURY
THE MANOR HOUSE MYSTERY SERIES

In WWII England, the quiet village of Sitting Marsh is faced with food rations and fear for loved ones. But Elizabeth Hartleigh Compton, lady of the Manor House, stubbornly insists that life must go on. Sitting Marsh residents depend on Elizabeth to make sure things go smoothly. Which means everything from sorting out gossip to solving the occasional murder.

A Bicycle Built for Murder
0-425-17856-0

Death is in the Air
0-425-18094-8

For Whom Death Tolls
0-425-18386-6

Dig Deep for Murder
0-425-18886-8

Paint by Murder
0-425-19215-6

Berried Alive
0-425-19490-6

Fire When Ready
0-425-19948-7

Wedding Rows
0-425-20804-4